A SPECTACLE UNTO THE WORLD

A SPECTACLE UNTO THE WORLD

The Catholic Worker Movement

TEXT BY ROBERT COLES

PHOTOGRAPHS BY JON ERIKSON

THE VIKING PRESS | NEW YORK

*To Dorothy Day, and all who have walked with her;
and to those many who have had the good fortune
to meet up with the "faith, hope, charity" of
the Catholic Worker movement*

For I think that God hath set forth us the apostles last, as it were appointed to death: for we are made a spectacle unto the world, and to angels, and to men.

We are fools for Christ's sake, but ye are wise in Christ; we are weak, but ye are strong; ye are honourable, but we are despised.

Even unto this present hour we both hunger, and thirst, and are naked, and are buffeted, and have no certain dwellingplace;

And labour, working with our own hands: being reviled, we bless; being persecuted, we suffer it:

Being defamed, we intreat: we are made as the filth of the world, and are the offscouring of all things unto this day.

I write not these things to shame you, but as my beloved sons I warn you.

For though ye have ten thousand instructors in Christ, yet have ye not many fathers: for in Christ Jesus I have begotten you through the gospel.

—I Corinthians 4:9–15

INTRODUCTION

WE HAVE APPROACHED THE IMPORTANT RESPONSIBILITY this book has been to us with a mixture of shyness and trepidation. Dorothy Day is a first-rate writer; in strong and clear prose she has poured out her thoughts and feelings so that interested readers might obtain a good idea of what the Catholic Worker movement has aimed at, hoped for, committed itself to doing. Father Alex Avitabile of Fordham University has compiled a bibliography of her writings, as well as those of men and women she has worked with, and one counts almost a hundred pieces, apart from all that she has written in *The Catholic Worker*, month in, month out. In addition, there are two autobiographies *(From Union Square to Rome* and *The Long Loneliness)* and two books meant to describe quite specifically what goes on in the life of this astonishing, self-effacing, yet proud movement *(House of Hospitality* and *Loaves and Fishes)*. Arthur Sheehan has written a lucid and suggestive biography of Peter Maurin, dead since 1949, and co-founder with Dorothy Day of *The Catholic Worker*. Maurin set down his own ideas in his various "easy essays," and they were nicely collected and arranged in *The Green Revolution*, with a touching introductory memoir by the woman he first met in late 1932 and eventually won over as a companion in a publishing venture that has, of course, amounted to something much more over the years.

Those years have piled up, too; this book comes out just after Dorothy Day's seventy-fifth birthday and on the fortieth anniversary of *The Catholic Worker*, which first appeared on May Day 1933. I hope that in the future social historians will bring their attention to the Catholic Worker movement, even as I expect that more and more personal accounts will be written by those who have labored in one or another way to bring its very special vision of man (and the Church's relationship to man) before people all over this nation. I hope, too, that a substantial biography of Dorothy Day will in time be written; Dwight MacDonald has made a poignant start in the two-part profile he contributed in *The New Yorker* (October 4 and 11, 1952) and in a follow-up piece for *The New York Review of Books* (January 28, 1971).

What, then, are we trying to do, Jon Erikson and I? We are not members of the Catholic Worker family, nor have we made an extensive investigation of its various religious and political struggles. We offer no thorough biographical study of Dorothy Day, either in words or photographs. I suppose it is best to say that we are a photographer and writer who have very much admired what the Catholic Worker movement has done, tries every day to do, has every hope of continuing to accomplish in coming years, and we wanted, with this book, to convey something of what we have seen and heard as observers of it. By the act of working on this book and, we hope, by the way we have done our work, we have tried to emphasize how significant we believe that movement is, how deserving of attention it is—especially from America's young people, who may not have had occasion to find out about this remarkable development in the history of the Catholic Church and of twentieth-century secular America.

Toward the end of the text of this book, I mention that I have for some time been in correspondence with Dorothy Day, and have come to talk with her and know her somewhat. When I decided that I wanted to write something about what I had seen and felt about the work she and her co-workers were doing, I became for a while paralyzed by an assortment of emotions. To put my hesitations and fears into questions: who was I, an outsider, a mere sympathizer and observer, to write about this tough, daring, and courageous effort being made silently and unostentatiously by so many men and women in different parts of the country? What purpose would my words fill, and for whose sake ought they to be set down? To answer those questions, partially at least, one can assign one's income from the book to *The Catholic Worker;* one can hope that its necessary and redemptive tradition would be a little strengthened by being made available to others, as a source of encouragement, as a means of self-definition, as an example of what has been and is still being done; and, finally, one can refer to one's own involvement with the Catholic Worker movement—as someone who worked alongside the men and women of it who came South in the early 1960s to act, and to act in response to a mandate from the conscience of a community of God-fearing but fearless social activists. (I believe I make clear, later in this book, what I learned in Mississippi from members of the Catholic Worker movement.) Still, one struggles with the knowledge that some are living out an impressive commitment, while others like me come by, watch, and listen, then move on to their stock-in-trade, words.

At last I could bring myself to discuss all of this with Dorothy Day and I must say I received from her little "understanding" or "sympathy," just a quiet demonstration of her impatience and annoyance with the kind of rhetorical and categorical and (thinly veiled) moralistic postures I was putting myself through and echoing from others—the likes of whom she has known all too well over the years.

"I am a writer, a journalist, you know," she started. "We are trying to do what we can," she continued, "and we began, actually, as a paper, *The Catholic Worker.* We hope to reach the people who read us, and we hope to reach the people who come here, to St. Joseph's House; we write because we want to share what we are trying to do with others."

Then, an hour or so later, when we had moved on to other matters, she came back to the subject: "We write in response to what we care about, what we believe to be important, what we want to share with others. I have never stopped wanting to do so. I have been reached so many times by certain writers. What is this distinction between writing and doing that some people make? Each is an act. Both can be part of a person's *response,* an ethical response to the world. I know that so much nonsense is said, is written. But a lot of nonsense is *done,* too—often by those who claim to know so much and be in the right about everything."

We went on, now talking about Jon Erikson's photography; she had seen some of it, and liked what she saw. So, though a photographic study of the Catholic Worker movement had not ever been done, and though she worried that it would be difficult (perhaps impossible) for someone to "come around with a camera and start snapping," she said yes.

She worried, I think it can be said, about the "method" of our project, not to mention our manners. What she told me, however indirectly and tactfully, was that she hoped, indeed *expected,* that we would behave ourselves, exercise care and restraint. The burden fell on Jon Erikson, because while I could go and talk with long-standing members of the Catholic Worker family like Pat Jordan or Jim Forest or Dorothy Day herself, and immerse myself in memories of experiences I'd had with other members, or read books and articles about the movement, Mr. Erikson had to be with, and eventually work with those on the front line, so to speak. He served coffee, helped make soup, tried to assist the badly upset, seriously confused, and hurt people who came in off the streets in search of—God only knows what, quite literally: everything from food and shelter and clothing to a chance for prayer, for solace, for self-examination; maybe, too, some came to begin a certain kind of undramatic resurrection, hard to sustain but moving to behold and even at times be part of, as Catholic Workers have been for these past forty years. One man who himself had a while back walked in "off the streets" and now was working in St. Joseph's House said of my friend and colleague—and this is only a small part of the testimony—"He's become part of us. He's been a great help to us."

Speaking of help, I must acknowledge gratefully and with affection the assistance of all those people I have already mentioned, and many others in some of the Catholic Workers' "houses of hospitality" that are to be found in cities all over this country. I would also like to acknowledge how much I learned when I spoke before a Friday evening meeting at St. Joseph's House in New York. That meeting, by the way, has become an institution of sorts, a weekly occasion for Catholic Workers to hear out and respond to those within their own ranks and others who might loosely be called "friends"—a description I have heard applied to visitors who come by to talk, but who also learn from their attentive listeners, an audience that generously and thoughtfully shares its rich and valuable experiences, acquired under circumstances that the friends often find hard to comprehend or, afterward, describe.

I want to acknowledge, also, the value of an evening I spent at Boston College, on April 13, 1972. For one week, teachers and students of that Jesuit institution dedicated themselves, one might say, to the Catholic Worker movement; they read and read, held discussions, collected money and clothing, and, most important for them, awaited Dorothy Day, who was to spend several days with them. She took sick, but they went on with their plans. I was honored to be asked to give a lecture on "Dorothy Day and the Catholic Worker" and especially honored on that occasion to meet a number of veterans of the movement. Their openness, kindness, and encouragement cannot be overstated; I was writing this book at that time, and, despite my conversation with Dorothy Day, was still apprehensive, if not despairing. Once again I was told to go on, and I have done so.

Finally, some explanations are in order. Jon Erikson has tried to capture some of the rhythm of the Catholic Worker movement. It is a movement that is concerned with charity and good works; it is a movement meant to express the personal and spiritual longings of many people; and, not least, it is a movement with its own ideology, a very special approach to politics and religious philosophy, and also to subjects and considerations now subsumed under words like "ecology" or "life-style" or the "counterculture." There is an irony, of course, to the presence among us of a somewhat older "movement" which has in countless ways anticipated what we today insist upon as being so new, so unprecedented, so contemporary. History is full of such ironies, though.

In any event, Mr. Erikson's camera has moved from a neighborhood, its streets and appearance, into a very particular scene; I believe he has done justice to the richness and complexity of it all—the place, the people, the work done, the ideals lived out. The text is meant to give readers some sense of what came together when Peter Maurin and Dorothy Day met and began their struggle (a lay apostolate of sorts within the Church) on behalf of the poor and oppressed of this planet. I have wanted to show, to some extent at least, what they brought to each other, not only as individuals but as representatives (as we all are, within limits) of larger social and historical forces. It is rare that a personal encounter becomes a moment in the social and political history of a nation and a church, but I do believe that the month of December 1932, when Dorothy Day met Peter Maurin, can be regarded as such. And, too, I try to give an account of what goes on during the days and nights when this complicated movement—like all movements never without its contradictions, inconsistencies, and ambiguities—tries to keep loyal to its high aims and hopes.

Unquestionably, other observers would choose to stress different aspects of the Catholic Worker movement. I make no claims for the "correctness" of the emphasis and tone I have supplied. I leave it for others to estimate the "success" of what Dorothy Day and so many of her spiritual kinfolk have done; those others will also no doubt try to fit the Catholic Worker effort more formally and methodically into the larger "frames of reference" one hears about from time to time. "We have been here," Dorothy Day told me once, "these past years, doing what we believed to be our duty, and wanting so very much only to be given the chance to keep on doing so. One can do what one can do; I think we all ought to remind ourselves of that every once in a while—because so often we turn on each other and demand or criticize, instead of looking back to ourselves, trying harder to remain faithful and true to the direction our own energies, our *soul,* has found suitable and valuable." At this point I can only repeat those words and let the reader move on to this particular response to a "spectacle" worthy, it can certainly be said, of Saint Paul's description.

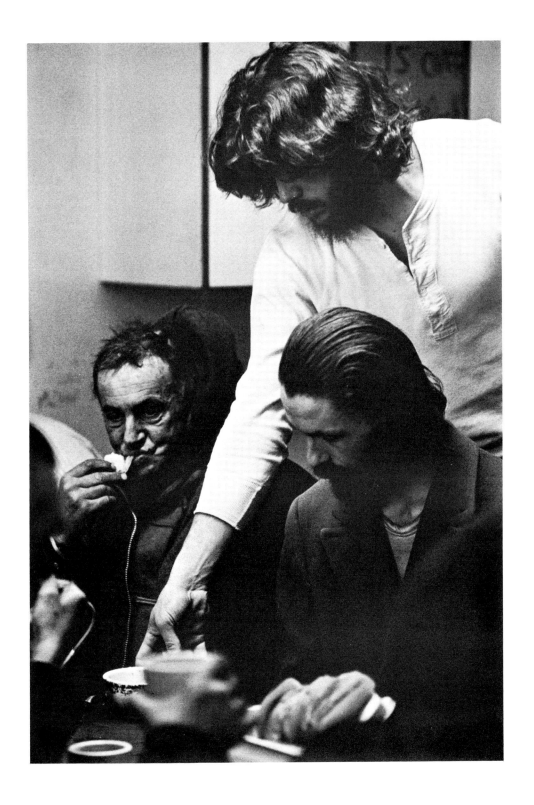

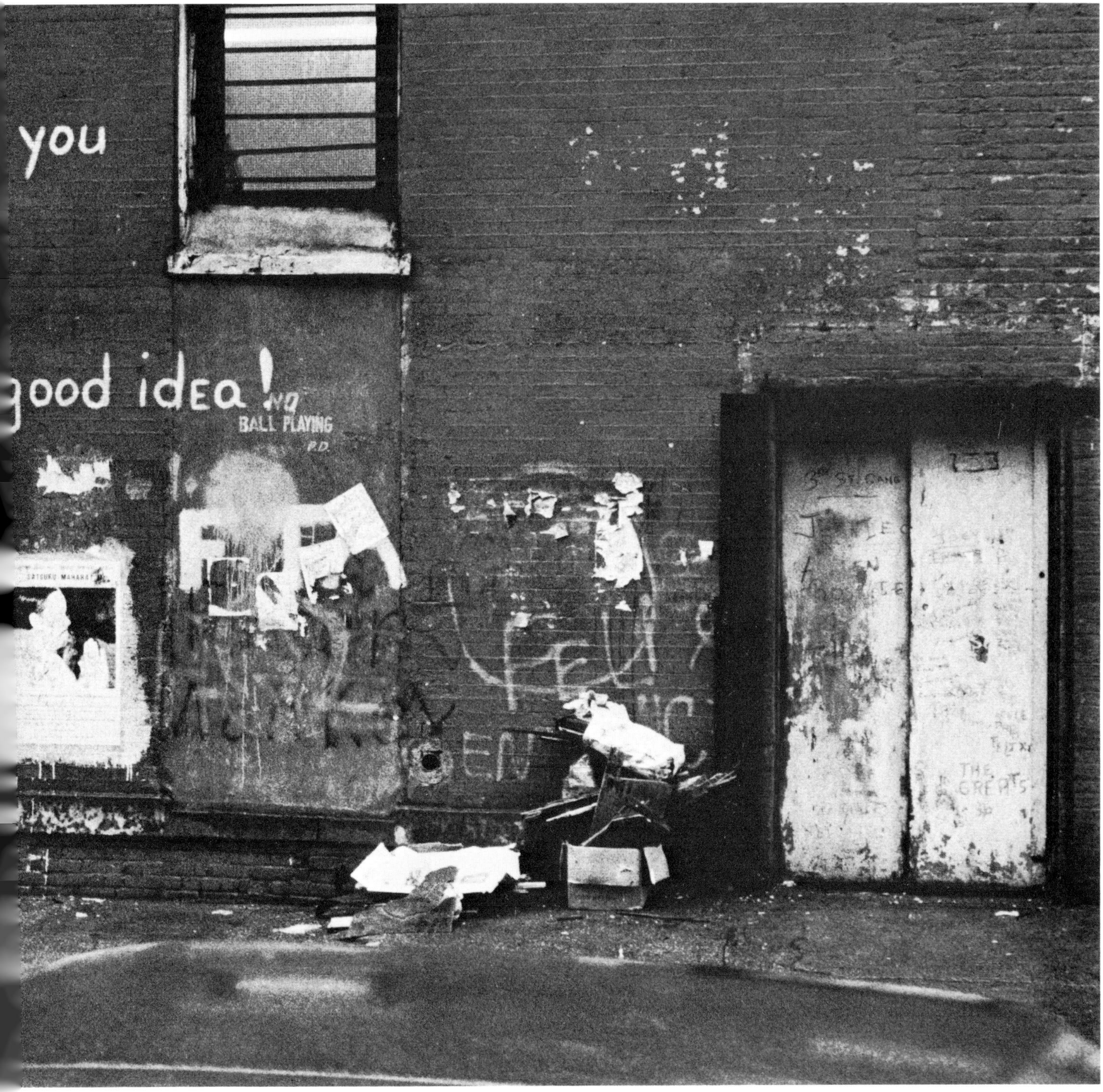
you
good idea!
NO
BALL PLAYING
P.D.

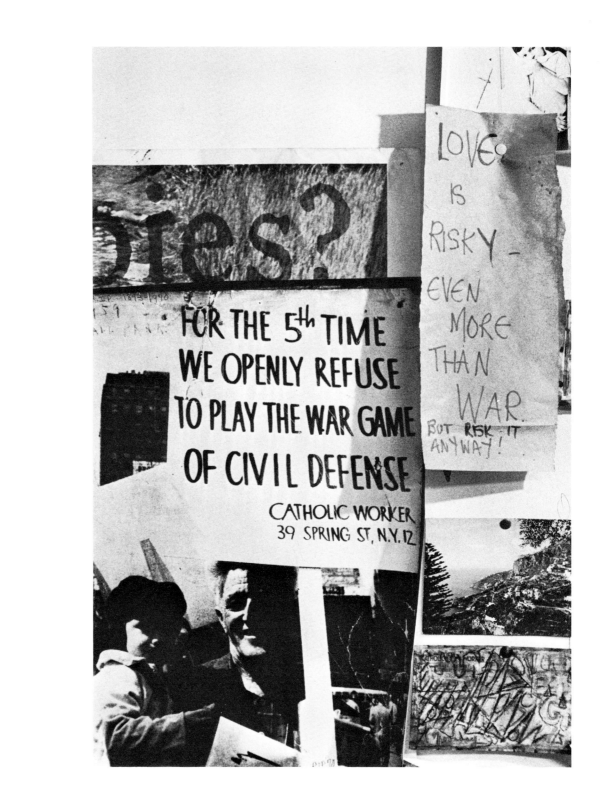

While imprisoned in the shed Pierre had learned not with his intellect but with his whole being, by life itself, that man is created for happiness, that happiness is within him, in the satisfaction of simple human needs, and that all unhappiness arizes not from privation but from superfluity. And now during these last three weeks of the march he had learned still another new, consolatory truth—that nothing in this world is terrible. He had learned that as there is no condition in which man can be happy and entirely free, so there is no condition in which he need be unhappy and lack freedom. He learned that suffering and freedom have their limits and that these limits are very near together. The harder his position became and the more terrible the future, the more independent of that position in which he found himself were the joyful and comforting thoughts, memories and imaginings that came to him. He had learned to see the great, eternal and infinite in everything... and gladly regarded the ever-changing, eternally great and infinite and unfathomable life around him. And the closer he looked the more tranquil and happy he became. That dreadful question, What for? which had formerly destroyed all his mental edifices, no longer existed for him. To that question, What for? a simple answer was now always ready in his soul:

LEO. TOLSTOY

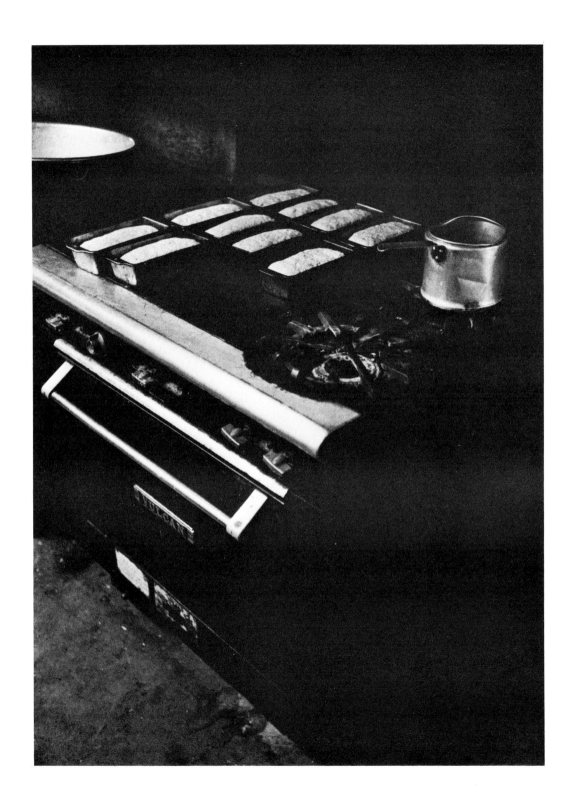

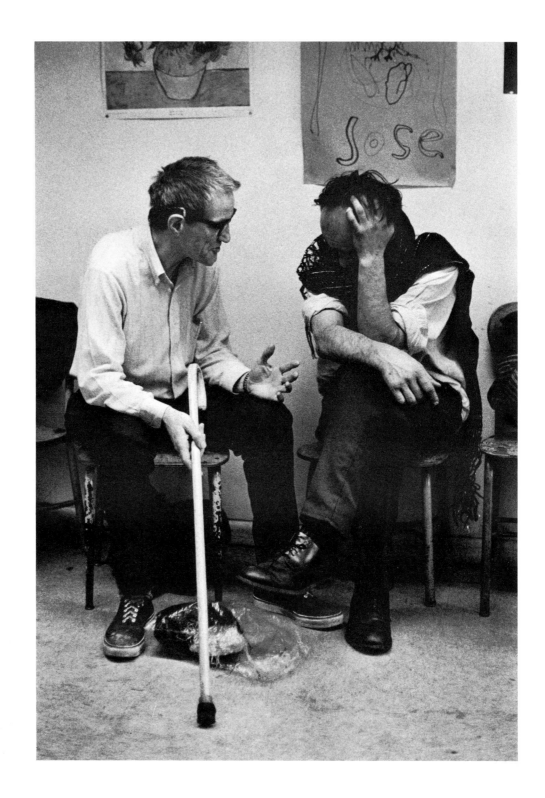

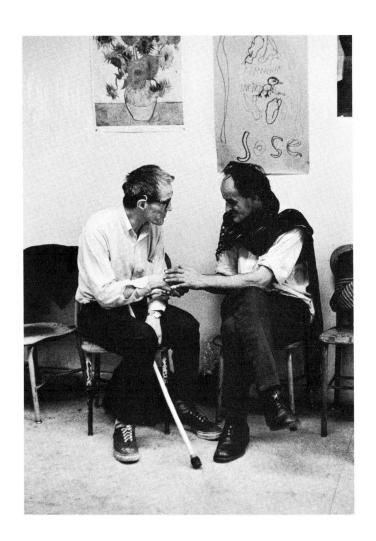

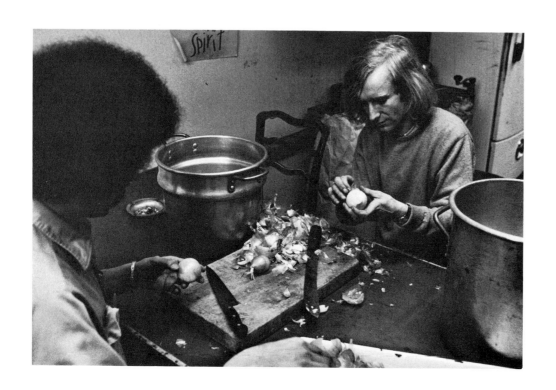

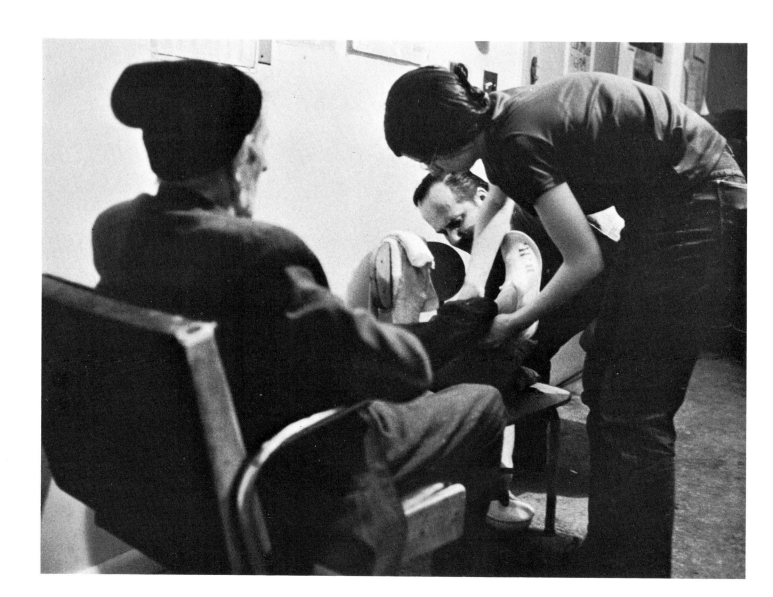

A SPECTACLE UNTO THE WORLD

CHRISTIANITY'S MOST SIGNIFICANT CONVERT, maybe its model convert, was Paul. "Saul who is also Paul" of Tarsus was no innocent bystander, suddenly and inexplicably singled out for attention by God's divine grace. Saul was an educated man, a young Pharisee who, before he became a Christian, was a passionately religious Jew, devoted to the Law and awed by it. Saul wanted to protect the Law against those who would usurp its traditions and its message; he was a loyal and obedient man of the empire and of his faith. More than that, he was energetic and zealous. He approached Damascus as a believer ready to do battle: the blasphemous require stern warnings and, if unrepentant, legitimate harassment by those who know how much they have to protect. His vision of the risen Christ, which took place on the road to Damascus, was not only momentary but ironic: Saul was traveling as a defender of God's Law, set down in the Torah; and this crucified Nazarene was not the first one to claim himself to be the Messiah, nor would he necessarily be the last; the true Messiah was to rise from the dead, be the one and only resurrected Prophet—and where was the evidence?

When Jesus as the Messiah came to Paul nothing spectacular happened. An already inward, dedicated man was loath to break with his past. Perhaps God's will preferred another, less dramatic, more demanding and complicated approach. Paul asked the Lord what he ought to do, and by implication was told; he "washed away his sins" and then went among his religious kinsmen, telling each and every one of them that he had been mistaken, that they were mistaken, that those unnervingly confident disciples of Jesus Christ were correct; they had indeed been with the Lord when He walked on this earth and in the end had been there to witness His ascension. Now was the time for others to step forth, for the Messiah must be acknowledged—by those whom God had all along chosen to do so, come the critical moment. If not Christ, who? If not right at this moment, when?

This effort of Paul's was not haphazard or of limited duration. The Pharisee did not turn away from the Law. He meditated. He visited one synagogue after another. He declared the Law newly ascendant, given an order of meaning only God Himself could bring—something long ago promised and at last brought to pass. Yet Paul was not a systematic thinker; if the continuities of the Old and New Testaments were going to be emphasized, he would not be the one to do the job in a well-argued, convincing way. Rather, he was to go back and forth, labor hard to persuade his fellow Jews that the old precepts were not enough, that a new kind of history had now begun to unfold—while all the while edging closer and closer to the Gentiles, to the Greco-Roman world of Corinth, Galatia, and Ephesus, and, ultimately, to the banks of the Tiber River.

It is quite difficult for us, twenty centuries later, to know what concrete, institutional arrangements Paul tried to live with, as well as struggle against. Today when we read him we take notice of his fiery evangelicalism, his determination that the letter of the law shall not be mistaken for God's spirit, as embodied by the experiences of Jesus Christ. For Paul, however, there were other preoccupations. In Jerusalem especially, Jews from various backgrounds had accepted Christ as the Messiah in the years immediately following His death, but in doing so they remained Jews culturally—paid dutiful adherence to the Mosaic Law and traditions. It was that community of Jews-become-Christians which Paul at once belonged to and challenged (the latter most especially when he insisted that Gentiles need pay no attention to Jewish customs when they accepted Christ's divinity). In A.D. 70 the Roman armies of Titus virtually destroyed Jerusalem and with it the power of this community; thereafter the churches of the Diaspora that Paul had done so much to help establish were on their own. But Paul was by then dead, a martyr to Rome's intense persecution of the early Christians. It is safe to say that Paul never really cut himself off from the church he knew, for all the strength of his personality and the force of his vision. His famous letters to the Corinthians, the Thessalonians, the Philippians, were meant to instruct those contemplating conversion as well as those he did convert, but they also show Paul addressing himself to the leaders of Jerusalem's Jewish-Christian community, who apparently could not easily forget or forgive his past as a persecutor of sorts.

I begin like this, with mention of Saint Paul and what he tried to do and was up against, because Dorothy Day is inclined to draw upon Saint Paul for courage and inspiration. In *Loaves and Fishes*, she writes, " 'A spectacle to the world, and to angels, and to men . . . the offscouring of all,' Saint Paul said, and that is what we became." But in addition, she and Peter Maurin in several important respects carry on a tradition Paul began, and some of the more puzzling aspects of the Catholic Worker movement can be better understood in that light, as yet another Pauline moment in the history of Christendom, wherein two Christians, one a man, a French peasant born to the faith, one a woman, an American convert, having been mysteriously brought together, set out to travel, write, and preach—in the interests of urging the most pointed and revolutionary changes upon all they encounter, while also working assiduously to stay well within the Church's fold.

The issue here is not loyalty to the Roman Catholic Church; it goes without saying that such loyalty was never in doubt for either Peter Maurin or Dorothy Day. Others have stayed in the Church as communicants yet moved further and further from their fellow members, not to mention from the hierarchy. Not so with Dorothy Day and her co-workers; they have maintained truly radical positions, especially extraordinary vis-à-vis their fellow Catholics, and also have located themselves spiritually (maybe the word is "socially" or "culturally") within the Church's mainstream. I think this ambiguity, one that Paul struggled with more strenuously than we now have any reason to know about, accounts for much of the strength and endurance of the Catholic Worker movement, and also for many of its apparent paradoxes, if not outright contradictions.

Paul attended to both pastoral and prophetic duties in an apparently natural manner that seemed as effective as it was unselfconscious. He pointed out directions, became a teacher, adviser, leader; at the same time he paid close attention to life's daily problems, no less important because they lack drama or fail to interest philosophers or theologians. He was an exceedingly agile fighter, who never wanted to make unnecessary enemies or lose sight of what he was after simply because he had become angered, disappointed, saddened for one reason or another. He could rail against those with whose beliefs or values he disagreed, then turn about and be temperate and judicious. A traveler, he could stay still, remain with a particular flock long enough to learn the rhythm of its everyday existence—a reality which for him was God-given, hence as instructive as any laws. A fighter, he could mediate, placate, move back and forth from Jerusalem's growing Christian church to the various settlements, nearby and far away.

If he strikes some of us today as moralistic and abusively puritanical, he was at heart the man who has lived a complicated and by no means consistent life. That is, Paul's "moralism" is not given self-righteously, from on high; a convert, a man who suddenly found himself wanting and wrong, he based everything on God's grace, and so the ethical precepts he offered were part of some larger, more generous scheme of things—God's "loving-kindness," for which one presumably makes sacrifices gratefully rather than desperately. His was the voice of a self-declared sinner. Like Augustine after him, Paul knew not to be complacent, knew and conveyed his precarious psychological and spiritual condition.

Peter Maurin and Dorothy Day had no doubt that they were among those who ought to heed Paul; each of them had a "past," and if neither of them had been bad persons, with a lot to live down, they both were seeking Paul's "new beginning" when they joined together in 1933—joined *forces,* perhaps, because the two were strong-minded, stubborn, and energetic beyond the capacity of most men or women. The elements they brought to their joint effort are astonishingly diverse—to the point that even a convinced realist might throw his hands up in the air and say yes, it probably was a thoroughly extraordinary encounter, a spiritual marriage of sorts that defies the most conscientious description or analysis. In any event, one tries to provide the description—recite the chronology, the personal histories, the social and cultural antecedents that came together in late 1932 and early 1933 in Manhattan's Lower East Side.

Peter Maurin had initiated the meeting, and to it he brought not only an exceptional life, but ties to the Catholic Church that in a way go right back to Saint Paul. The Rome that Paul wanted to win over was the Rome that ruled the land which is now the Languedoc area in the southern part of France. Peter Maurin was born there on May 8, 1877, in the mountain village of Oultet; his family had owned a farm nearby for over fifteen hundred years. That is to say, not long after Paul's death the Christian faith began to take hold among the "barbarians" Rome had fought so hard to subdue. In time, families like the Maurins—uneducated Gentiles, people of the earth, and far away from Christ's Nazareth and Jerusalem—became the ardently believing mainstay of the Holy Roman Church.

Not that Languedoc's villagers and farmers have nourished any lively and commanding philosophical or theological tradition within the Church. They have often been compliant, the people of the French land—those with an eye for politics correctly refer to the reactionary, benighted, superstitious peasantry, always at the mercy of the exploitative petite bourgeoisie, which has itself so often just left the land for the villages and towns whose markets and stores and schools (not to mention churches) draw families from miles and miles around. Historians have often ignored such places; history is made in Paris—ideas are generated there or come from elsewhere in the country to gain sanction, and power is located there. In those small settlements, removed from city life, one can feel the centuries slip away; what remains is almost but not quite timeless —the land to be mastered, year in and year out, children to be raised, God to be worshiped—and, of course, ignored too, even by the most devoted. Georges Bernanos has described the life in *Diary of a Country Priest* and, more tragically, in *Mouchette:* the narrowness and boredom that can inform the lives of hardworking farmers and, as well, their decency and kindness and generosity; the burden of tough, demanding labor, and at the same time the utter necessity of it, not only so that people can eat and be clothed, but so that the meanness and pettiness we all must struggle with somehow become tamed, victims of the exhaustion each evening brings. But the fearful, joyous presence of the Catholic Church—Her rituals, Her authority—is unavoidable. Towers announce Her; bells insist upon Her right to summon anyone and everyone; schools are devoted to Her, never stop bringing children further and further into Her fold; men of the cloth, women in the habit, give of themselves to Her in dozens of ways, marry Her, sing Her praises, fight for Her in wars only generals might not recognize— the soul is a battleground, the soul is won or lost, evil is an enemy whose chameleonlike ingenuity and resilience can never be overestimated, and on and on the military imagery goes.

I suppose Peter Maurin's life risks being considered "archetypal." He was one of twenty-two children. (His father's first wife died, leaving two boys and a girl; a second marriage brought forth an uninterrupted procession of children.) He grew up planting, weeding, harvesting, close to the land and close to the animals which live off the land. He was lively, hard-working, idealistic. He eventually joined the De la Salle Brotherhood, taking his first annual vows in September 1895. The Brothers would never achieve priesthood. They taught and, especially, made an effort to teach the children of the poor; for doing so they wanted no honors, no privileges, even within the Church. Blessed de la Salle, after whom the order took its name, was not unlike Paul in several respects: a most devoted Christian, he was an educator and, very important, he emphasized the value of children being taught in their native tongue, rather than in Latin or Greek. Maybe at any given point in history there are those who feel themselves securely in possession of *the* laws, *the* tongues—and also those who dare to raise their voices on behalf of everyone: the poor, the unlettered, the unnoticed, the far from elect. Peter Maurin, eager to help the needy he knew well in Languedoc, learned to be a teacher. But then he was sent to Paris, of all places, where he found himself for the first time up against the profoundly anticlerical spirit of the times. Even within the Church there was substantial conflict: between those who were loyal to the Republic and those who were royalists or unashamedly authoritarian; between those who wanted to emphasize Christ's universal ministry and those who connected everything and everyone, Christ Himself included, to *patrie*, the nation-state as a universe all its own; and, not least, between those who chose to emphasize and work to undo injustice and those who accepted (maybe embraced) class and caste as givens not to be tampered with—lest hungry, atheistic hordes be let loose and a whole way of life (if not a "civilization") be ground under.

In the late 1890s Marc Sanguier, a brilliant and devout Catholic student, had succeeded in founding the Sillon movement—an effort at religious renewal on the part of thousands of French youth. Unquestionably the movement was nourished if not directly inspired by the encyclical *Rerum novarum* (May 15, 1891) in which Pope Leo XIII had emphasized that "labor is not a commodity." The Holy Father had appreciated the significance of what those around him ignored—the power of various modern secular philosophers, the departure of many intellectuals from the Church, a drift of the urban masses toward religious indifference if not outright atheism, and an equation established in minds of more and more people of Catholicism and the economic-political *status quo*. The encyclical was, for the time, a striking departure from the policies and pronouncements hitherto formulated in the Vatican. Naturally, the family was defended against secular onslaughts, but the right to own things, the right to acquire more and more, was given a very definite context. If religious institutions were to be defended by the state, if a degree of property was also to be protected by every government, then parliaments and representative assemblies had other obligations as well: to intervene on behalf of the working-man and the poor; to encourage and strengthen the weak as against the rich and powerful by securing the right of laborers to organize and demand their just share of money and influence.

Now, some eighty years later, Pope Leo's message may not seem surprising or exceptional, even as many of the conditions Dorothy Day and Peter Maurin saw about them in 1933 are no longer so prominent a part of our lives in this country. In the 1890s, though, the higher ranks of Europe's Catholic world were scandalized by the Pope's abrupt turn toward the "lower orders" of society. But Pope Leo's position gave strength to the Sillon movement, to men like Peter Maurin who joined it in order to change the social order while retaining their religious faith.

By 1903 Maurin had left the De la Salle Brotherhood. Under their auspices he had worked with orphans and abandoned children in Paris and had felt of some help to the most vulnerable and hurt, but he wanted to do even more. Caught up by the reformist spirit within the Church, he wanted to be part of a kind of lay ministry to Paris's sorely aggrieved poor.

For six years Peter Maurin worked in the Sillon movement. What he would later do in the Catholic Worker movement was anticipated by his actions as a Sillonist. He lived with the poor of Paris. He talked of their plight to people wherever he could find them. He spread the "good news" Pope Leo had sent forth. He could be found every day on the street—often in front of Notre-Dame—urging passers-by to buy *L'Eveil démocratique*. As a news seller he was one of the *Camelots du Sillon;* their counterparts on the right were known as *Camelots du roi*, whose paper was Charles Maurras' *L'Action Française*. There were arguments, even brawls between the two groups, a reflection among the "lower" cadres of the intense political and philosophical struggle going on within the French Church. Members of the Sillon organized public meetings, cooperatives, all sorts of leagues, committees, unions. In addition, there were a magazine, several other newspapers, and—most significant so far as the history of the Catholic Worker movement goes—rest homes: eating places, where the poor and their advocates from other segments of the population could come together; and a hospice or two set up to receive the homeless and penniless, those aimless wanderers which any large city possesses and chooses to ignore or hound or try to care for.

The Sillonists soon enough succumbed to the suspicions and fears of France's guarded and self-protective bourgeois laity, well endowed with influential friends in the Vatican. Not that the kind of social and ethical concern advocated by men like Peter Maurin was explicitly part of the Socialist or Decentralist or Distributist movements. One senses in *le Sillon* a sincere, middle-class effort to heed the Gospels, pursue Christ's life-long interest in the destiny of the poor. Perhaps what was lacking was a political leader willing and able, at the very least, to heed Christ's warning that guile would be required by those who worked on His behalf. In any event, the essentially "personalist" (as Maurin later called it) approach of the Sillonists stirred thousands of people to idealistic action—but in the clutch failed to change French social and economic institutions. The enthusiasm and generosity of spirit mustered by young people were no match for the power of the industrialists, the landed gentry, the firmly entrenched if nervously insecure bourgeoisie, and the assorted politicians, generals, and, yes, bishops who listened attentively to them all. So it was that a man like Peter Maurin, however devoted he was to the pacifist spirit of *le Sillon*, could not escape the recurrent calls to military service that were required by a militarist nation, at that time bent on acquiring colonies all over the world, and soon to wage a war to the death (to the death of millions) against Germany, an increasingly successful competitor.

By 1907 Maurin had more or less decided to leave France for Canada, where no military service would face him. In 1898 Canada had received Russia's nonviolent, devoutly religious Dukhobors, whom the Tsar had brutally persecuted and Tolstoi had ardently championed. (Fittingly enough, the royalties from *Resurrection* had gone to them.) Canada had space available for homesteaders, and many thousands of French-speaking people. Maurin said a long good-by to his beloved family and to the South of France he had so recently been away from.

As he prepared to leave he began reading Kropotkin—*Field, Factories and Workships* and *Mutual Aid*. The emphasis in those books is on the redemptive as well as utilitarian value of family, of community farms, and of small home crafts. Industrial workers had become "alienated," Kropotkin pointed out, agreeing with Marx. But not only industrial workers. Kropotkin saw *all* men as rootless—removed from the land, cut off from their own potential capacities as builders, makers, artisans if not artists. Once, the eye had staked out a task and hands worked to accomplish it. Once, men and women planned things, worked at them, finished them, and saw themselves as useful and creative human beings every single day. They were people who planted seeds and harvested crops, or fashioned things out of clay, wood, leather, and metal—things to use or to look at and enjoy. Now there were assembly lines, and instead of individuals or families, crowds were cut off from other crowds, with everyone at the mercy of assorted strangers, often perceived as enemies. Perhaps Kropotkin romanticized the ancient Greeks and the medieval age; perhaps, when we marvel at what was accomplished by this or that man or by certain guilds, we ignore the collective misery, even the slavery, that was also to be found in those earlier times. Even so, much has been lost as well as gained in the name of progress, and men like Kropotkin, Tolstoi, and Maurin were not willing to submit themselves and their fellow men to some "dialectic" of progress in human history, supposedly relentless and inevitable in its workings, and maybe, at bottom, a religious construct, albeit to the Christian a pagan one. The point was to draw upon the values and practices of other centuries and establish them as alternatives to at least some of the apparent necessities and urgencies of an altogether new phenomenon, the capitalist nation-state.

Before he left his native land Peter Maurin began the kind of itinerant life he was later to pursue for so long in Canada and the United States. He went from town to town, stopping here and there to talk with people and learn from them how they thought they should live their lives, what they wished their beloved France *might* one day become. He slept inside or outside, whatever suited the given day's circumstances. He sold tea, coffee, cocoa—to earn just enough to feed himself and not become an object of curiosity or notoriety. (His family was not far away from the countryside he took as his home.) Then in 1909 he left France, never to return. He crossed the Atlantic and crossed most of Canada, heading for the wheat fields of Alberta Province. A friend with whom he hoped to homestead was killed in an accident, and out of loneliness and sadness Maurin gave up the idea of settling in one place and began wandering again. He dug ditches. He quarried stone. He worked as a harvester. He joined teams of construction workers. He drifted across the border to the United States, begged his way through New York, New Jersey, Maryland, and Pennsylvania, where he was arrested for vagrancy. In western Pennsylvania he worked in a coal mine. After a while he moved on to a lead mine near Dubuque, Iowa. Next came a trip to Chicago—free, because he rode the freight trains.

(He was arrested for doing that, too.) Later came St. Louis and a stint in a syrup factory, followed by a return to Chicago and a job as a janitor.

In 1925 Peter Maurin came east to New York City, and shortly thereafter went through a period of religious introspection and self-scrutiny. What was he, a believing Catholic, to do with his life? A man of enormous energy and vitality, keenly interested in people and how they so variously manage to make do, he felt himself called to yet another kind of lay apostolate. He continued moving from town to town, now mostly in New York State, but once again he had a message to offer, and he seized any and every chance to do so. He spoke to priests, to Rotarians, to somebody of importance, to any nobody he would meet while walking the roads. He began writing the essays that one day thousands would read in *The Catholic Worker* and in his book *Easy Essays*. The sentences would be brief and emphatic; he would repeat himself just enough to make a strong impression on the reader or listener, but the repetitions would also be amplifications, and the arrangements of the sentences would be poetic—a few words on one line, the end of the sentence on the next, then a very brief statement followed by a much longer one, usually broken up into phrases calculated to stand on their own as well as fit into a larger declaration.

We ought all to try hard to go back to the land, he argued. We ought to live together as members of a social and religious community that transcends all those categories that keep people apart—social class, the several races or religious denominations, those arbitrary lines that set off one village from another, and on and on. We ought to give of ourselves to each other, work not for money but because we want to join hands with friends and neighbors in a common pursuit of a decent and dignified (and religiously grounded) life. Not least, we ought to begin in small ways, with specific, concrete actions.

Maurin was a thinker, full of ideas and theories, some of them utopian, some of them sensibly practical. Yet in his everyday life he spent day and night with ordinary men and women who were simply trying to get by, survive today so that there would be a tomorrow, never mind a next month or year. Those hard-pressed and more than likely exhausted people lacked Maurin's abstract sympathy and outrage; they seemed to tether him to the actual tasks that needed to be done, thus undercutting his natural inclination to speculate, as a thinker or theorist so often does, oblivious to what is going on outside the library or study. Not that he didn't keep on writing on the larger issues that faced America and the world in the late 1920s, and he read hungrily, especially lay Catholic periodicals. When he wasn't preaching to others or himself, he became part of someone else's audience, including among others Dorothy Day's. She had been writing for *Commonweal, The Sign, America,* and before that, *Socialist Call* and *The Masses*; she had written a novel; she had covered a whole range of political events as a reporter. Now she had in Peter Maurin an unknown admirer: he found in her recent writing (1931–32) a familiar and welcome mixture of religious and political sensibility. George N. Shuster, then editor of *Commonweal,* had also noticed the similarity of views between the two writers, and suggested to Maurin that he look up Miss Day and spend some time talking with her. Never shy or hesitant when *ideas* were at stake, when some *action* might come out of this or that effort, the itinerant pamphleteer, orator, worker, man devoted to God, took his friend's advice.

T HEY FIRST MET in December 1932, five years after Dorothy Day had been baptized a Catholic. She had just returned from Washington, D.C., where thousands of desperate citizens had taken part in the Unemployed Councils' Hunger March. She was there as a reporter, but also as a woman who for years (even before her conversion) had worked for social and political change. Most of that work was done alongside ardent Socialist and Communist friends—men and women who saw the United States as a country controlled by powerful bankers and industrialists, for all the pieties one heard about "freedom" and "democracy" and "the rights of the individual." After her conversion she became a very religious person; one might say that much of the energy and passion she had found for secular matters was now given over to prayer and meditation. But by no means did the Catholic Church serve as an "opiate" for Dorothy Day. She continued in the late 1920s and early 1930s to be absorbed with the difficulties faced by the poor and vulnerable people of this nation, so many millions of them. Though the mother of a young girl, she went to observe the struggles of workers to organize, of the hungry to obtain food and work, and wrote about what she saw. Her prayers were meant to be a prelude to action, yet in late 1932, as the country lay prostrate and the government seemed utterly helpless and, worse, disposed to cover up its helplessness with displays of panicky brutishness, those prayers seemed to have gone unanswered. Dorothy Day was an experienced and able journalist, and she could have continued to write about the various tragedies and disasters that America seemed destined to experience without letup from 1929 until, of all things, a world war put an end to the nation's economic Depression. She wanted to do more, though. On December 8, 1932, perhaps in response to what she had just seen on the streets of the nation's capital—fiercely proud men, hungry for bread and work, petitioning their elected representatives, and being treated as the scum of the earth for doing so—she had taken herself to the National Shrine of the Immaculate Conception at Catholic University: "There I offered up a special prayer, a prayer which came with tears and anguish, that some way would open up for me to use what talents I possessed for my fellow workers, for the poor."

When she returned to her child (and brother and sister-in-law, who were staying with them) Peter Maurin was there, waiting to exchange ideas with her, waiting to urge a course of action upon her. She, in turn, was more than ready to respond—and in retrospect has come to think of all her earlier life (she was then thirty-five years old) as a preparation for that encounter. Not that she had lived a very thought-out or conscientiously dedicated life. She was born on November 8, 1897 in the Bath Beach section of Brooklyn. Her parents were not at all religious: neither her mother nor her father attended church, though her mother had been baptized an Episcopalian and her father came from an Episcopalian family; none of their children were baptized. Her father's family were Southerners, from Georgia and Tennessee; grandfather Day had been a surgeon in the Confederate Army. Her mother's family traced itself back to Upstate New York and various parts of Massachusetts. When she was six years old her family moved west to Berkeley, then to Oakland, California. Later on she recalled reading the Bible somewhat furtively up in the attic, and (at eight) going to a Methodist Church with a friend. Then in 1906 the San Francisco earthquake occurred; among the buildings destroyed was that of the newspaper for which Mr. Day worked as a sports editor. The family abruptly moved back east, this time to Chicago, first the South Side of the city, later on the North Side. The home was comfortable, but certainly not luxurious.

As one goes through Dorothy Day's recollections of childhood and youth the thoroughly, almost prototypically American quality of her background comes across quite strongly. The family's roots were imbedded in both the North and the South; the family had lived in the East, the West, and the Midwest. It was neither a rich nor a poor family. The Days were not churchgoers, but Mr. Day could be seen upon occasion with a Bible in his hands, and he often quoted from it. The family was not highly "educated," certainly not "intellectual," yet no "picture books" or detective stories were allowed in the house—only Scott, Hugo, Dickens, Stevenson, Cooper, and Poe. The family was not concerned with social or political issues, though Mrs. Day had a vigorous sense of what is right and what is wrong, which she communicated to her children; and Mr. Day laced his writing about racing and race tracks (he was one of the founders of the Hialeah track in Florida) with strongly moral quotations from the Bible and Shakespeare. And

Dorothy met with no objection from her parents when she chose to attend church. For that matter, in Chicago the Days allowed their sons to join the choir of a small Episcopalian church on the South Side—and their sister Dorothy rejoiced at the sight and sound of them.

Moreover, there were those stray books or singular episodes that together go to make up an inheritance of sorts, however subtle or implied rather than spelled out: a volume of John Wesley's sermons that "happen" to be in the house; the arrival of a Christian Science practitioner, with her *Science and Health with a Key to the Scriptures,* and just as important, her unqualified conviction that Mrs. Day's severe and apparently intractable headaches would quite definitely and promptly yield to the faith of a believer; the presence nearby of a devoutly Catholic mother, or an insistent Episcopal minister, or a school friend who waxed lyrical over Biblical passages and who (a certain kind of twentieth-century skeptic would add) poured into the Sunday morning hymns and prayers all kinds of adolescent sentimentality, if not passion. "All beauty, all joy, all music thrilled my heart and my flesh, so that they cried out for fulfillment, for union." When Dorothy Day writes that way about her adolescent religious stirrings she is quick to add that some of Saint Augustine's writings deeply influenced her at the time—not because that kind (hers, his) of religious passion now strikes her as "immature," drawing as it does upon the body's sensuality, but rather in recognition of a certain fellowship she once experienced as she went through some of the doubts and struggles Augustine acknowledges so pointedly. Like him, she knew for years how far away it was: the particular "fulfillment" she would keep on seeking—no matter how unconventional or uninhibited a life she might lead.

She did defy conventions, too—and began to do so rather early, when in high school and still living at home. Her challenge to her parents' somewhat staid and conformist ways was done under the thoroughly American aegis of writers like Carl Sandburg, Jack London, and Upton Sinclair. She began to forsake Lake Michigan and the lovely, unspoiled parks that rimmed it for other parts of Chicago—the West Side, with its poor immigrant families: Poles, Germans, Italians, Irish, all worse off than she, and in their own ways fascinating to a growing woman of her background. They appeared so robust, so firm in their beliefs, so set in their habits. If they were poor and at the mercy of all sorts of exploiters, they nevertheless seemed to have an enviable sureness about them—those many churches, so heavily frequented, and the markets, bakeries, and taverns in and out of which large families flocked, noisy and sometimes strangely dressed and full of life. She may have romanticized Chicago's slums; some would say (even today) that she has persisted in doing the same with New York's slums when she marvels at a lone tree in back of a grim series of tenements; or when she is quick to notice the sight of a flower, however lonely and beaten down by the city, and quick to pay attention to "the smell of lumber, of tar, of roasting coffee"; or when she admires the warmth and kindness of the city's poor, of people who have seemed (even to her, at various points in her life) fearful, suspicious, and calculating or ungenerous to one another, never mind outsiders. Still, like the rest of us she has never been able to forget what she was taught as a child, and it is against that earlier attitude that she has had continually to struggle: "From my earliest remembrance the destitute were always looked upon as the shiftless, the worthless, those without talent of any kind, let alone the ability to make a living for themselves. They were that way because of their own fault. They chose their lot." And of course they were said to drink and carouse and waste everyone's time. For that matter, if they were sober and hard-working, there must be some larger, some divinely inspired reason for such a state of affairs. Hadn't Christ Himself said that the poor would always be with us? Hadn't He told His followers that His kingdom was not of this world? So why worry about here-and-now poverty when a whole new and eternal life can be hoped for, prayed for, fervently (maybe desperately) believed in?

Dorothy Day was not able to shield herself from the implications of questions like these; in fact, when she arrived at the University of Illinois she joined the Socialist party precisely because she could not be satisfied with the inhumanity she saw around her, and by the same token she could only feel contemptuous of the willingness so many ministers have to interpret Christ's life and message as an almost infinite justification for the *status quo*. For her "the lame, the halt, and the blind" must be made well, strong, and clear-eyed. For her there was *this world,* in all its injustice and crying need for reform; and the more drastic and thorough the reform was, the better: "Jesus said, 'Blessed are the meek,' but I could not be meek at the thought of injustice." She favored the angry, defiant Jesus, ready at long last to drive the moneylenders from the temple. She favored secular saints, men like Eugene Debs and the Haymarket Martyrs, who had been framed and put to death in 1887. She favored the "Molly Maguires" or the Knights of Labor, workingmen who had the gall to believe they were entitled to an eight-hour day and a strong union. In sum, she felt drawn to America's populist tradition, with its emphasis on class consciousness, egalitarianism, and militant political action.

She stayed at Urbana for only two years, but they were critical ones in her life. She kept company with the campus radicals, immersed herself in the literature of social protest and revolution, felt herself "in love now with the masses." She was a great one for all-night discussions; she had an extraordinarily open mind and sought out those whom others of her militant background might well have shunned: avowed Socialists and Communists; intense intellectuals; activist and cosmopolitan Jews who by and large kept to themselves and were looked down upon by many of their fellow students. She began to write. She began to learn how political organizations work. She began to become part of a small and informal but distinct community whose members shared her idealism and her outrage at what obtained in Woodrow Wilson's America, despite the President's call for all sorts of reform.

By 1916 Dorothy Day was in New York City, working as a reporter for the *Call,* a Socialist paper. As in Chicago, she wandered the streets of Manhattan tirelessly. When she writes about those first months on the *Call* (she was not yet twenty) she brings to mind Orwell's accounts of his life in Paris and London as a "down and out" observer and essayist. She was keenly interested in everything and everyone: the rich and the poor; the lonely and the large immigrant families who crowded into the city's tenements; the busy, alive quality one feels; and the sad moments that never stop coming up—if one only cares to pay attention. She was all over the place, to some extent because her job required it, but also because she was hungry for the city's sights and sounds, which at least temporarily appeased her urgent desire to learn all there is to learn about the way people live. She went to strike meetings and watched picket lines and attended peace meetings and met people, and more people, all sorts of people, working-men and -women, pacifists, anarchists, Christians, atheists, writers, storekeepers, men dazed by alcohol or by the despair they felt for themselves and their families. She read pamphlets put out by the I.W.W. and articles written by American and European Socialists or Communists. When an appeal or a protest was made, she was there. She followed marches, covered street-corner meetings. She met Trotsky before he returned to Russia, rejoiced in Madison Square Garden on March 21, 1917, when thousands assembled to hail the success of the February Revolution. Eventually she became involved with *The Masses;* she knew and worked with Mike Gold, Max Eastman, Floyd Dell. She met John Reed. She lived for a while on MacDougal Street, helped give breakfast, lunch, and dinner parties—and the talk was endless, serious, and argumentative. One senses in Dorothy Day's descriptions of those times a mixture of sheer youthful exuberance, unconnected to any philosophical or ideological pursuit, and the intensity that radical politics can generate in men and women who are willing to devote themselves to a tough and unpopular struggle against the relatively stable political system of the United States. One minute Dorothy Day and Mike Gold are singing revolutionary songs at the end of a pier or savoring the Manhattan sky-line, the next they are getting ready for exactly what they were shrewd enough to anticipate, the massive repression a wartime nation would impose on Pacifists and Socialists.

The federal government could stop publication of *The Masses,* but it found other dissenters a greater problem. In 1917 Dorothy Day went to Washington with the suffragettes and was jailed. It was not to be the last time she would find herself in a cell. She did not go as an outspoken advocate of women's rights: "It was mainly because my friend Peggy Baird was going that I decided one evening to accompany her." The reader of her book is often in this way asked to believe that she almost drifted into some of her most demanding and sacrific-ing efforts. Whatever her motives, she stayed with her fellow women, was pushed about, insulted, humiliated, kept in a wretchedly overcrowded cell, and made to feel like some sort of moral monster—all because she held to the belief that women ought to be able to vote. I think it is fair to say that she has gone through a succession of similar experiences throughout her life: what others (the so-called "majority" or the "authorities") at a given moment consider to be a wild scheme, or terribly radical, or not only illegal but immoral, is vigorously sup-ported—only to be accepted at a later date as pure common sense.

After she came out of prison she returned to New York and apparently went through a period of aimlessness. She moved from job to job, was not sure what she wanted to do, where and with whom she wished to live. She spent a year training to be a nurse at Kings County Hospital in Brooklyn. She loved the work, felt exhausted by its demands, and finally quit because she could not suffer the discipline required, and the routine pettiness some of that discipline amounted to. At the time she simply may have been unprepared to devote herself single-mindedly to any person, place, or job. For a while she worked on the *Liberator,* successor to *The Masses.* She spent a good deal of her time in the Provincetown Playhouse, talking with Eugene O'Neill, Terry Karlin (an aging Irish anarchist), and again, Mike Gold. Upon occasion she would pick up the Bible, only to put it down. Mostly she was interested in writing and political reform. Her friends continued to be writers, artists, and, always, radicals ill at ease with the assumptions of a capitalist society. She went to Europe for a year, spending time in England, France, and Italy. Later she apologetically noted how insulated she was as a tourist; she had many radical *ideas* about what a good society ought be like, but as she moved across the Continent she kept the company of intellectuals and saw little of what was actually happening to ordinary Frenchmen or Italians. Upon her return to America she went to Chicago, picked up with her friends from the I.W.W., and was again arrested and sent to jail, now with a number of Wobblies during the "red raids," when, as she put it in retrospect, "no one was safe." Needless to say, millions of Americans were safe, all too safe; they were not Wobblies, and if there was a good deal of latent populism in them, it was never going to get in Attorney General A. Palmer Mitchell's way. The point, of course, is that all along she was taking for granted a certain position she had assumed in relationship to the prevailing economic and political orthodoxies. (In that regard, for all the drama of her religious conversion, she has remained very much the same person: from Warren Gamaliel Harding to Richard Milhous Nixon she has expected no safety. And maybe she would want to point out that her antagonists, too, have not been all that different over the years.)

Through Harding's Presidency and into Coolidge's, while the nation returned to "normalcy" and Wall Street began to enjoy its seemingly endless boom, she lived well on the periphery of Main Street. She took temporary writing assignments, did proofreading, worked in a library, was a cashier in a restaurant, became a clerk in a Montgomery Ward store. She posed for art classes. She did a series of news stories on Chicago's courts—the children's court, the domestic relations court, the so-called morals court. (Ben Hecht and Charles MacArthur were friends and fellow reporters, doing the kind of muckraking journalism she has always felt drawn to.) Meanwhile, one gathers (from the autobiographical comments she made later on, after her decision to join the Church) that she fell in and out of love, not often but enough to feel, upon occasion, old while still young. Her reading at the time was serious, and maybe not of the kind that young, educated Americans (even more, radical ones) usually read: Pascal's *Pensées* and, periodically, sections of the New Testament.

For a few months she went to New Orleans, obtained a job with the *Item*. She lived in the French Quarter, enjoyed its good food, wrote several articles on the lives of dance-hall girls, and, for some reason, kept going to the nearby St. Louis Cathedral. A friend even gave her a rosary, but the time had not yet come for it to be used. She had written a novel, *The Eleventh Virgin*, and while in New Orleans learned that the motion-picture rights had been sold for $5000, no small sum in 1923. Her mind was more and more intent on writing; if she was not especially drawn to the Church, she was even less drawn to political activity. With money at last, she could leave New Orleans, return to New York, and obtain a house on the beach in Staten Island, where she hoped to continue and expand her career as a serious writer.

We are now at a critical point in her life. It is 1925 and she is approaching thirty. She has fallen deeply in love with a man she only refers to as Forster. At one point she describes him tersely this way: "The man I loved, with whom I entered into a common-law marriage, was an anarchist, an Englishman by descent, and a biologist. He was also a Southerner, having been born in North Carolina and educated in Georgia and Virginia." In many respects he was an agrarian, and indeed he and Dorthy Day came to know the Allen Tates—and the Malcolm Cowleys, the Kenneth Burkes, and Hart Crane and John Dos Passos. She is both respectful and mildly ironic, if not openly wry, when she describes those heady days in New York, when she would stop writing, leave her isolated place on Staten Island for Greenwich Village, and, with her friend Forster, join what she called a "set." "They reminded me of Samuel Johnson and his crowd," she observes tersely. Then she adds: "I can remember one conversation among Malcolm, Kenneth, and John Dos Passos which stood out especially in my memory because I could not understand a word of it." Kenneth Burke, for instance, whom she obviously respected and liked, is mentioned this way: "At that time Kenneth was translating, editing the *Dial* and writing the first of his strange books." She is being, as she often has been, disarmingly candid, willing at any cost, it would seem, to expose her own naïveté, if not acknowledge her ignorance and lack of education.

After all, she just *happened* to know a suffragette, hence the trip with her to Washington and eventual arrest and imprisonment. In Chicago she *innocently* went to see Wobbly friends, hence her arrest a second time at the hands of a government anxious to uncover "reds" wherever they might be living, or better, be *said* to live. But her friends all seemed to know what they wanted out of life: they were writers or artists, or they were avowed Communists or Socialists or Anarchists. They made approximations about the meaning of the present and foretold what the future (more or less imminent) would bring in the way of upheaval and revolution. But Dorothy Day alternately turned on herself, taking all too careful note of her inadequacies and weaknesses, or lived quietly by the ocean on Staten Island, reading Tolstoi, Dostoevski, and Dickens.

She also began "consciously to pray more," to read the *Imitation of Christ,* and she resumed writing a diary, which she had from time to time kept since she was a child. Forster worked in the city during the week, spent weekends with her. She has poignantly described the happiness they experienced together, culminating in the birth of their daughter Tamar Teresa in March 1927. They were now a family of three, though not recognized as such either before God or by man's laws. Shortly after Tamar was born her mother wrote an article for *New Masses* describing the experience she had just gone through—the joy she felt, and the gratitude and the sense of awe. Yet Forster did not see things as she did. He was gloomy about the world, to the point that he questioned whether children ought to be brought into it. When Sacco and Vanzetti were executed he was virtually destroyed psychologically for weeks; he became silent, went off by him-self for long stretches, and seemed to have given up all interest in life. All the while his infant was there, being cared for by her mother—and being prayed for, too.

I suppose one could come up with all sorts of psychiatric speculations about what went on between Dorothy Day and Forster. Maybe one could even try to explain her conversion as a response to the difficulties she went through as a friendship became a romance, a romance turned into a common-law marriage, a marriage bore forth a child—and relentlessly the child's parents seemed to become more and more estranged. Not that they argued that much; as one reads Dorothy Day's several accounts of her life with Forster, one can only take note of the way two people could come together and find love for each other, and then begin to separate, less out of mutual annoyance or anger, less in response to disagreements (however real and substantial) than out of separate inabilities to break faith with themselves. I used the word "faith" because in several ways it seems to describe what was at issue between the two of them—or maybe, better, the four or six or eight of them. Often Dorothy Day makes mention of the various parts of herself: she could be bold and rebellious, but then find herself repelled by the Bohemian frankness of others; she could see the hypocritical and superstitious side of religious practice, but stop short of outright atheistic scorn—and suddenly, for no apparent reason, even find herself on her knees praying, or reading Thomas à Kempis or Saint Augustine, not to mention the Bible; she could love her intellectual friends, take pride in the friendships she had with them, yet in a flash tire of, then be outraged by their wordiness and self-centeredness. "This exaltation of the articulate obscures the fact that there are millions of people in this world who feel and in some ways carry on courageously even though they cannot talk or reason brilliantly. This very talk may obscure everything that we know nothing of now, and who knows but that silence may lead us to it."

She wrote those words while carrying her child, whose very name gives further expression to ambiguities that have never, in certain respects, been "resolved," perhaps simply and directly turned to good account. Tamar, which in Hebrew means "little palm tree," was the name two of her intellectual Jewish friends had given their daughter, and she liked it; Teresa was originally meant to be in honor of Teresa of Avila, though Saint Thérèse of Lisieux—the little Teresa, the Little Flower—was summoned for additional help: to be the child's "novice-mistress." ("I wanted both saints to be taking care of her. One was not enough.") There she was, feeling that way—though not yet baptized herself, never mind the infant.

We know now what happened. We have a word for it, "conversion"—even as we can say, with all our psychological sophistication, that the parents of little Tamar Teresa had serious "problems" and for that reason eventually had to separate. Nor would Dorothy Day deny this to have been the case, though she would perhaps prefer to talk about differences in temperament—if indeed she had any interest at all in labeling the complicated and valuable qualities possessed by two distinct individuals with a series of psychological or psychiatric terms. In fact, the two loved one another very much, learned from one another, together shared a kind of thoughtfulness and a basic decency that transcended the egotism we all must struggle with. They were also in many respects incompatible: one was a naturalist, a pessimist, an atheist; the other was endlessly interested in and involved with the world, incurably hopeful about people and their possibilities (without being given to whistling in the dark) and haunted (I believe that is the correct word) by the thought of God.

Dorothy Day makes it clear that in the final analysis she had to choose between Forster and her increasingly insistent and unyielding religious convictions. "I wanted Tamar to have a way of life and instruction. We all crave order, and in the Book of Job, Hell is described as a place where no order is. I felt that 'belonging' to a church would bring that order into her life which I felt my own lacked." Doubtless there were "tensions" between the two strong-willed friends, and doubtless in response to their gradual estrangement, Dorothy Day felt all the more strongly the lack of order, if not outright disorder, in her own life.

At this point one gets ready to leap forth with a more far-reaching ("comprehensive" it might be called) interpretation—and it would not be very original, even as it would beg as many questions as it seemed to answer. A woman who had already lived several lives, who had traveled all over, met so very many people, experienced her fair share of hardship, gone to jail, felt lonely and uprooted, become separated in so many ways from her family and its values, was at last and surprisingly (to her) fulfilled as the mother of a child. But she had to face, maybe for the first time in her life, the implications that a newborn baby presents to all parents. Now I cannot just pick up and go here or there. Now I have to think of more than my own life; there is before me, before *us*, the long stretch of days and weeks that go to make up a daughter's "childhood," her "youth." Now I will have to think about questions that a child asks, about the worth of my own ideas—do I want to see them taken up by another?—and not least, about those unstated assumptions which govern all households, and maybe more than anything else influence the way a growing child thinks and feels.

Tamar Teresa, Dorothy Day knew, would soon enough begin looking around and taking notice and accepting the values and purposes her particular world happened to urge. I live here rather than there, the child would eventually learn. I have been told this and not that. We do one thing, but not another—and on and on. Is it really all that surprising to find at this moment heightened religious and philosophical concerns in a sensitive, socially conscious, introspective woman, a thoughtful writer and political observer, a seeker and a bit of a wanderer, an outgoing yet in some crucial sense lonely woman, aware that (so far as a father for her child goes) she might soon be alone? Indeed, it is hard *not* to dwell on the psychological significance of Dorothy Day's conversion. When I learned from her books that Forster's "extreme individualism made him feel that he of all people should not be a father," I wondered whether she didn't also feel that way—whether she had not, as she took on the responsibilities of mother-hood, struggled (in the form of a stormy religious battle) with precisely that kind of individualism. And when I came across her saying about Tamar, "I knew that I was not going to have her floundering through many years as I had done, doubting and hesitating, undisciplined and amoral," I found my mind registering its not very surprising (these days) connections—they may be appreciated by some as banalities: the Church will be a mother and a father to this new and anxious mother, soon to be forsaken by Forster; the Church will give this some-what rebellious and anarchic spirit (well, of course, it is *minds* we are talking about) a home at last, a home in which, finally, she will really feel at home, therefore able to offer one to her daughter.

I shall not burden the reader with the technical language that psychiatrists have come to use as we go about submitting others (and ourselves) to this line of reasoning, nor will I deny that for some people at certain moments, a con-version can turn out to be rather more a psychological than a spiritual turning point—even here the arbitrariness of the distinction is misleading—and so po-tentially suspect. Any experienced minister or priest knows this. What I really have to ask myself, and ask so many of us who body and soul belong to this secular society of which psychiatrists have become so prominent a part, might be put this way: why do I pay so close attention to the emotional nuances of Dorothy Day's conversion, and every day fail to wonder about the mothers and fathers who do not embark on the kind of serious and sustained soul-searching she experienced and later wrote about? Who deserves special scrutiny, the Dorothy Days of this world, or the rest of us, who seem so sure of ourselves, so confidently able to move on from one psychological hurdle to another, who bear and bring up our children without much evidence that we have gone through agonies, spent days or nights asking ourselves (with a desperation utterly in keeping with the state of the world) *why, how, what for?*

Before moving on, then, to what *came* of this particular religious conversion, to what has since given so many people an occasion for gratitude, one must take note of the length and depth of the spiritual self-examination Dorothy Day put herself through as she prepared to make her first step toward the Catholic Church. Moments of skepticism and confusion were to be expected. Mixed feelings were natural. But at times she felt torn apart; she loved a man who had no use for a faith she was powerfully, urgently drawn to—and, indeed, her daughter's father was prepared to leave if it came to that, her declaration of belief. The mother, taking child in hand, made a decision she at times must have tried to put off on the basis of every possible excuse. Something in her could not be put off; something prompted her to read William James's *The Varieties of Religious Experience,* accounts of the lives of Saint Teresa of Avila and Saint John of the Cross; something required her to go back to the New Testament and her well-thumbed *Imitation of Christ.* Still, when she finally took the three Sacraments—Baptism, Penance, and Holy Eucharist—she was grim and somewhat forlorn. Especially, she felt self-conscious. She didn't entirely disbelieve what she had heard Forster say about churches and those who go to them—and she loved him.

Moreover, "there was another love, too, the life I had led in the radical movement." As she moved ever closer to Rome, she worked even harder on behalf of those whose commitments she has summarized geographically as "Union Square." Newly a mother, a fresh convert to Catholicism, she was also interviewing workers, talking with the unemployed, and writing up what she saw and heard in her own style—strong, forceful description, mixed with a nicely controlled but by no means disguised expression of moral outrage. "I was working with the Anti-Imperialist League, a Communist affiliate," she points out, and she wanted to be doing just that; her Communist friends this time, as on many other occasions, were on the side of Nicaragua's poor who were making a last-ditch (and doomed) effort to overthrow a clique of powerful landowners, many of them United States-connected, who virtually owned that banana republic. How was she to reconcile her nascent religious faith, with her knowledge that in so many instances the Church betrayed Christ, was allied with people who were mean and cruel and greedy (and rich and powerful)? She was no clever, self-deluding, and self-serving apostate, ready to forget the poor and take up with those who can pay handsomely anyone who will work for them, maybe write for them now and then—and do so under cover of a burst of piety, suffused perhaps with evasive but high-sounding flights of religious fancy. If anything, she was getting more radical by the year. Nor was she able to contain herself as she looked closely at the American Catholic Church. "Where were the Catholic voices crying out for these men?" she asked, thinking of Sacco and Vanzetti. "The worst enemies will be those of our own household," Christ had felt it necessary to say, and she could not put the remark out of her mind.

She left Staten Island, and with Tamar settled into a place on West 14th Street "in order to be near Our Lady of Guadalupe Church." She prayed often—long and hard. She steeped herself in theological reading. She talked almost daily to her confessor—and was still at sea, for all the anchor the Church had become for her. All the while she kept up with her old friends. The confessor, Father Zachary, wisely told her to keep her "Communist job" until she found another one. She went as often as she could to see Eva Le Gallienne's troupe in an old theater across the street from her apartment. She had many of the company over to dinner again and again. She obtained another job, with the Fellowship of Reconciliation, once more trying to fight injustice, once more working closely with non-Catholics. She wrote a play; it looked promising to various directors and producers—and soon there was a contract with Pathé, followed by a trip to Hollywood and a brief career as a film writer. In no time she was ready to leave California. She had enough money to spend a few months in Mexico, and did so, staying with a poor family in the capital. Living was cheap there, she wanted to stay longer; but Tamar became ill and they returned to New York.

The stock-market crash of 1929 had been followed by increasing economic decline, in turn followed by widespread social unrest throughout America. People everywhere were losing their jobs. Families were being evicted. Businesses were closing down. Farmers were near bankruptcy. Riots were breaking out. Meanwhile, the government stood by, its leaders either well meaning but confused and lacking in courage and determination, or else unwilling to break with the past. In the face of all this, Dorothy Day "felt out of it." In a brief and tactful way she noted how many groups of people were moved to take action, and then added: "There was Catholic membership in all these groups, of course, but no Catholic leadership. It was that very year [1929] that Pope Pius XI said sadly to Canon Cardijn, who was organizing the workers in Belgium, 'the workers of the world are lost to the Church'."

The woman who took note of that remark was now getting ready to do some "organizing" of her own. She was going to Mass daily, reading a substantial number of "spiritual books"—but also keeping up with her old radical friends. In 1932 they joined hundreds of others in Union Square to start the Hunger March to Washington, and with them, as an observer, traveled Dorothy Day. (In order to do so she put aside a second novel she was writing, one she would never complete because its subject matter would become the living substance of her life—"a social novel with the pursuit of a job as the motive and the social revolution as its crisis.") She was "lonely, deadly lonely" but, one suspects, not because she lacked friends and in any way failed on her own part to respond to them. Women, she felt, or at least the kind of woman she knew she was, "must have a community, a group, an exchange with others." They want a vocation, she insisted—yet at every turn they are denied the possibilities of such fulfillment, and are berated, to boot, by blind, self-centered, and self-righteous men and women. These people who have decreed themselves (and obtained the power to be) judges of who may or may not walk with head up, stomachs full, mind and heart allowed free rein—these people have every reason to watch out for Teresas of Avila and Dorothy Days, for the women who affirm themselves by upholding *everyone*'s right to live free of the absurd and killing constraints various societies choose arbitrarily to place upon its members.

Just before she went to Washington on the Hunger March—and ended up praying to God that somehow, in some capacity, she might find a way to work with the poor in His Name—Dorothy Day read again and at some length about Saint Teresa of Avila. Once more I must insist that I have no interest in coming up with psychological formulations about Dorothy Day's struggles as a woman. I do, however, believe that Saint Teresa's influence on Dorothy Day was decisive. Both of them wanted to reform existing institutions and do so in a thorough, *radical* way, and each of them, as women, went through the hardest and loneliest of struggles. Saint Teresa hovered over Dorothy Day as she began to seek the means of taking up an extraordinary effort, both religious and social, on behalf of others. And in the paragraph that ends the introduction to *House of Hospitality*, Saint Teresa also is permitted to speak, loud and clear, and to this age's sensibilities, most instructively.

If our Lord should give me grace to say anything that is good, the approval of grave and learned persons will be sufficient; and should there be anything useful, it will be God's, not mine; for I have no learning, nor goodness. . . . I write also as if by stealth and with trouble because thereby I am kept from spinning; and I live in a poor house and have a great deal of business. If our Lord had given me better abilities and a more retentive memory I might then have profited by what I heard or read, and so, if I should say anything good our Lord wills it for some good; and whatever is useless or bad, that will be mine . . . in other things, my being a woman is sufficient to account for my stupidity.

Dorothy Day has so often remarked upon the special wisdom novelists possess and convey to the rest of us, and I think it is useful at this point to call upon a woman novelist. Here is how George Eliot chose to begin *Middlemarch*, her "study of English provincial life"—its nineteenth-century, Protestant variety, of course:

> That Spanish woman who lived three hundred years ago, was certainly not the last of her kind. Many Teresas have been born who found for themselves no epic life wherein there was a constant unfolding of far-resonant action; perhaps only a life of mistakes, the offspring of a certain spiritual grandeur ill-matched with the meanness of opportunity; perhaps a tragic failure which found no sacred poet and sank unwept into oblivion. With dim lights and tangled circumstances they tried to shape their thought and deed in noble agreement; but after all, to common eyes their struggles seemed mere inconsistency and formlessness; for these later-born Teresas were helped by no coherent social faith and order which could perform the function of knowledge for the ardently willing soul. Their ardour alternated between a vague ideal and the common yearning of womanhood; so that the one was disapproved as extravagance, and the other condemned as a lapse.

A woman of strong and willful disposition, Saint Teresa knew how to be practical and resourceful. She could have her mystical moments, but inevitably they seemed to give way to the earthy common sense that a person bent on changing things here and now on this earth must have. Disarming in her candor, she could also be shrewd—and a tough organizer, willing to give orders and see that they were obeyed. She desired to set down for others how the soul moves closer to its fate, union with God, but she never lost sight of the institutions and individuals (a whole world of Catholicism, in jeopardy as it faced the Reformation) she wanted to affect. One cannot know how seriously (in the passage Dorothy Day quotes) Teresa intended her humility to cast such devastating and unfair reflection on herself and her fellow women—but if one makes reservations for a given period in history, one ought also keep in mind a writer's guile, a fighter's natural shrewdness, her ability to disarm her foes by appealing to their excesses of vanity. Nor is this the place to explore the significance of George Eliot's extraordinary prelude. "Young and old, even in the busiest years of our lives, we women especially are victims of the long loneliness," wrote Dorothy Day. I need not analyze the common hurdles and conflicts those three women, born in different centuries and nations, had to face. They were each especially gifted and no doubt their respective situations were unusual; most women, like most men, are not destined to be saints, great novelists, or founders of significant social and religious movements. On the other hand, each of these women, sensitive as they were to the *human* issues at stake in their work, had to insist that there was something especially difficult and burdensome about their condition *as women*. Today they would probably write about that condition differently; the almost mocking self-effacement of Saint Teresa, George Eliot's bitter irony, Dorothy Day's expression of regret, all might give way to a more direct and open kind of social criticism, tempered perhaps by the inherent modesty of all three, but made strong and sharp by their awareness of scandalous injustice.

Dorothy Day and Peter Maurin spent December 1932 and the first months of 1933 getting to know what each other believed and wanted to do in the years ahead. At one point in *The Long Loneliness*, published in 1952, she indicates that Peter Maurin's "spirit and ideas will dominate the rest of this book as they will dominate the rest of my life." Rather obviously, her spirit and ideas would decisively change, if not "dominate" the rest of his life, too. In fact, an almost miraculous interaction of psychological elements, of social and cultural antecedents, occurred.

Peter Maurin took the initiative; he was the wandering scholar, the man seeking a means of offering a lifetime's accumulation of knowledge and experience to others. In him were to be found the European Catholic Church: he had been a Brother, and also part of an important lay effort. He was also the teacher, the restless social observer, the man who had not only "worked" with the poor but been one of them. Arrested as a vagrant, used to flophouses, indifferent to worldly things, he concentrated his vision on the evils of this world—as Communists had often put it, "man's inhumanity to man." He even claimed the Church's prior right to "communism"; Christ and His disciples surely had no vested interest in capitalism or colonialism. It is an awful paradox: Christian, "civilized" nations of Europe prospering from the brutal exploitation of millions of men and women. Nor is anyone in a drawing room of London, a Paris *salon*, and, yes, a church in Rome, all that likely to make the connection—between murderous servitude and a whole standard of living enjoyed by the burghers of so-called enlightened countries. No wonder one of Christ's first public acts was to overturn the tables of the moneychangers. No wonder Saint Paul railed against those who hide behind the letter of the law—while all sorts of devilish wrongdoing is permitted by the most insistently pious of men, whose showy piety in no way diminishes their greed and callousness.

After Saint Paul was converted, he took to the road, a "new man," hopeful as never before. He took stock of his enemies, and maybe even a few who declared themselves "sympathetic," if not willing to join him outright—and went on his inspired way, a man almost madly sure of himself. In similar vein these two new friends, Dorothy Day and Peter Maurin, began to believe (imagine the brashness, the plain nerve, the feigned innocence which in the Bible is called "guile") that they, virtual paupers, unconnected to people of "influence," could do something, and do it then and there, when a giant of a nation was on its hands and knees and maybe even dying, for all anyone at the time knew.

They certainly did a lot of talking before they acted. Dorothy Day refers to the "indoctrinating" she received from Maurin. I would suspect that she also had a thing or two to say. The man was convinced that now was the time, this was the place, here in New York City—to address Catholic workingmen, to speak out boldly to the Catholic unemployed, to work away at the conscience of the Catholic rich, and, beyond that, to come forth with a larger message aimed at the industrial West's people, of whatever religious, racial, or cultural background. He was full of ideas, given to abstractions, bursting with programs. She was resourceful, sensible, quick to figure out the concrete approaches, a useful and practical beginning, a plan of operations. Peter Maurin wanted to call the paper they talked about starting *The Catholic Radical*, but Dorothy Day preferred *The Catholic Worker*. Peter Maurin wanted to emphasize his belief that more and more "round-table discussions" were needed (so that people could be persuaded to take a good, long, hard look at their society), as well as houses of hospitality and "agronomic universities," where increasingly rampant and destructive industrialization would be countered by students learning how to work the land and become more nearly self-sufficient. But Dorothy Day would insist, as she has many times, that "I speak as the conventional American, in spite of years in the radical movement," and she worried that some of his ideas, interesting and worthwhile though they were, would not strike a responsive chord in the ordinary American workingman. The result, naturally, was give-and-take: the paper would be *The Catholic Worker*, Peter Maurin would contribute his broad-scale "easy essays," full of historical and philosophical analysis, all couched, however, in language anyone could understand; on the other hand, there would be a good deal of writing about the immediate problems at home—the Depression's disastrous impact on the everyday life of America's people.

The Catholic Worker first appeared on May Day 1933. Its text was typed, then taken to a printer who received $57 for putting out 2500 copies of what Miss Day later described as "a small eight-page sheet the size of *The Nation.*" The money came from one of the two founders (Peter Maurin had no money, Dorothy Day was working at odd jobs and so had a few extra dollars) and from two priests and a nun. Initially there was no office, no promotion, no staff, no mailing list; even when the monthly paper's circulation later soared to one hundred thousand, then one hundred and fifty thousand (in a matter of a year or two), things were done casually, informally, noncommercially. Woodcuts by Ade Bethune or Fritz Eichenberg, strong and powerfully symbolic, eventually began to grace the pages. Articles were written by those who in growing numbers came to be part of the movement. But in the beginning there were just a man and a woman and their handful of friends—writing copy, making up the paper, selling it on the street (not infrequently to the scorn of Union Square's radicals who couldn't for the life of them figure out what had happened to Dorothy Day).

I have just referred to the "movement"; in an astonishingly brief period of time, months rather than years, what was begun as a stab in the dark, a paper "backed" by nothing but "a pair of fools"—Saint Paul's "fools for Christ's sake" —turned into just that, a movement, a lively, yeasty, social, and political effort. Its influence over the years cannot be conveyed in the conventional manner: dollars and cents, the circulation of a paper, laws passed, citations or medals or awards won, honorary degrees obtained. For the fact is that in 1933 the American Catholic Church had been unable to respond to the sorely felt needs of its members, so many of them blue-collar workers who lived in the nation's larger cities. It had only recently ceased to be a source of inspiration and support for immigrants; by the 1930s it was becoming settled and established, even as millions of Irish, Italian, and Polish families became proudly and self-consciously American in allegiance. If the nation was paralyzed politically—it was in conservative hands yet desperately needed radical social and economic policies—Catholics were offered no religious context in which change could be attempted. Not only were their bishops cautious—no great surprise anywhere—but in the lower ranks of the Church those priests and nuns who had daily reason to know how many of their parishioners were penniless, out of work, hungry, could do virtually nothing. There was no real tradition of Catholic social activism in America, which clergy and laity alike might call upon and add to or modify in keeping with the awful circumstances of the moment.

Of course, in every century and all over the world the Church has never simply stood there, a force above and beyond man's temporal world. Nor has it had, less grandly, only an educational and moral influence upon its members, who are then free to live other lives, as voters or workers or residents of this or that neighborhood. The Church has always wedded itself to the lives of its people, and as a result, like all institutions, it is claimed, contested, fought over bitterly, circumvented, persuaded, lobbied, and pressured. In a sense, the Church has from the very beginning been a battleground. And what is won can be lost; Popes change, and with them come and go subtle inclinations or decided turns of direction. While certain assumptions are held to be fixed, for the humble and faithful of this world and for those whose religious faith constantly meets up with the actuality of life in dozens of imperceptible ways, the shifts within the Church have an important meaning. It is a meaning that gets lived out rather than analyzed or even prayed over.

How the Church chooses to look at its social mission becomes for millions of devout believers a signal: whether one must put up with things as they are forever; or whether one can and should, with God's sanction no less, begin to look for alternatives, and, once found, organize and act to realize them. Rather obviously, given enough desperation some of the faithful will wander away from the Church; neither the French Catholic Church nor the Russian Orthodox Church could prevent revolutions, whatever "hold" both of them had on the hungry, desperate millions of France and Russia. Still, as Dorothy Day knew well, the Church, for whatever reasons, can substantially help the landowners and big businessmen and generals in their mission to stay on top, even as a strongly reformist Church can inspire people to demand for themselves—demand the kind of care and concern Christ demonstrated to the poor, to the weak, and to the scorned.

No wonder *The Catholic Worker* caught on; and no wonder Dorothy Day and Peter Maurin were soon joined by countless friends, sympathizers, admirers—and people in great need. One suspects that at that point, within weeks of the paper's first appearance, Dorothy Day really came into her own. She had all along been a journalist, and would never stop being one. Peter Maurin had come to her because he knew she was an able writer, and sensed that she could tie his ideas down to the requirements of a newspaper or give them—in what way he perhaps did not at first know—the wider exposure he believed they urgently deserved. She, in turn, had by that time no illusions about the printed word; she had been writing for years and had become a very good writer indeed. But she was also a recent convert, a woman with a young child, a person of lifelong religious sensibility now intent on devoting her considerable energies to the needs of those who had much less than her. One suspects she wanted a larger family for herself and her daughter, a family spiritually bound to the Church yet on its own, a family that would draw upon and nourish her particular gifts—as a writer, as a woman interested in politics, as a person deeply offended by the injustices that millions had to pay for with broken, shortened lives, as a reader who kept learning from the lives of the saints, as an intellectual of her own special kind.

From the start Peter Maurin had talked to Dorothy Day about hospices or houses of hospitality, places where "works of mercy" could be offered and ac-knowledged in a person-to-person fashion, free of the faceless, bureaucratic procedures that govern the "welfare-state" notion of what ought to be done for (and to) the poor. But like everything else that developed out of the Catholic Worker movement, there was no grand design, no elaborate program that en-visioned x "centers" located in y cities at z cost. Peter Maurin harked back to the earlier years of Christianity, when bishops and lay people had taken per-sonal responsibility for those in dire straits; one way they had done so was to establish and run places (hospices) where the needy could be offered rest, food, clothing, a place to pray and collect oneself, so to speak. As *The Catholic Worker* grew, some extremely down-and-out people came by to be of help. They needed food or clothes. Some of them even needed shelter. Still, they wanted to give, to aid a fledgling Catholic effort at reform. They belonged to the 13 million un-employed America could then boast of. Casually and naturally all those involved in making the paper a periodical reality shared things with each other and their visitors—money, food, clothing. But in a matter of a few months it was clear that something more formal had to be set in motion. So, apartments were rented, coffee and bread and butter and soup were served.

Within a few years there were thirty-three houses of hospitality and farms in the United States. Over the years they have opened and closed. The hospices have started here, moved there, stopped for a while, appeared again. The pages of *The Catholic Worker* always emphasized the importance of agriculture, both for the obvious purpose of growing one's food and as an antidote to the excesses of industrialism, wherein man is separated from all purpose in life other than the demands of the assembly line. And farms also were built up by the men, women, and children who were part of the Catholic Worker movement—in New England and New York State, in Appalachia, in the Mid-West, and on the Pacific Coast. As these centers of action spread, these knots of kindred souls, other papers began to appear; they were sold along with the "main" *Catholic Worker,* published in New York City, in Chicago, Buffalo, St. Louis, Seattle, and as far away as England and Australia. There was no party line, no effort to make each hospitality house, each newspaper, conform to certain rules or positions. What thousands of men and women all over the world responded to was the brave determination of Catholic laymen to heed once again Christ's message, so often muted if not turned into a caricature of itself by those who ran the churches, among others.

The Catholic Worker movement was not simply the result of determined leadership finding a wide and persistent response in extremely desperate times. Dorothy Day and Peter Maurin were especially drawn to Saint Paul, and I believe they recognized in him a particular kind of disciple—eager to strike out boldly in the interests of a belief, but aware constantly that a fiery reformer needs "guile," as Christ said, if he is not to find himself or herself cut off from the people who most need saving. So, Paul not only reached out for the Gentiles but concerned himself with his own kind, the Jews who constituted most of the membership of the early Christian Church. That is to say, he wanted to breathe life into a church, not pull it down—in which case, naturally, there would have been him and him alone. History reveals him as apostle to the Gentiles, but to be that apostle he had to mediate between the Gentiles and a given institution—the tradition of Jewish Christianity, centered in Jerusalem.

By the same token, Dorothy Day had moved "from Union Square to Rome," and she had every intention of staying put, once and for all, come what may. She was not about to become a spiritual Protestant of sorts, or a nominal Catholic, or a secular activist using the Church as a tactical base of operations for getting to a notably reserved, indifferent, or suspicious "constituency." She was, is, will never stop being a devout Catholic; maybe these days she seems a sentimental and old-fashioned one to those within the Church otherwise sympathetic to her social and political aims, or to those outside who call themselves agnostics or atheists yet feel themselves comrades of hers in a common struggle against capitalist (and state capitalist) exploitàtion. Peter Maurin, too, was deeply of the Church; he brought to the Catholic Worker that strain of Catholic social concern that easily goes back through Chesterton and Hilaire Belloc to reformers like John of the Cross and Teresa of Avila, not to mention Francis of Assisi—each of whose ideals, also, have been as watered down, rendered inert, desecrated (by being turned into catch phrases or high-sounding homilies, to be repeated but not actively heeded) as have Christ's own sermons.

One could go on and on, trying to connect the Catholic Worker movement with other social movements, other political philosophies, other deeds initiated at various moments in man's history, or other ideas formulated both within and outside of the Catholic Church. Anarchism, distributism, personalism, communitarianism, Christian socialism, a kind of primitive "Catholic communism," pacifism, Prince Kropotkin, Eric Gill, Gandhi, Lanza del Vasto, Danilo Dolci; the words and names pour forth, and in the end there is only a continuing demonstration of Christ's spirit. Mountains have not been moved, nations have not been seized. If attention has been paid, obscurity and derision have also been forthcoming. No doubt about it, the movement has had its difficulties and limitations, some of them known to its members, even proclaimed by them. In that sense the movement has aimed to be exemplary, maybe confessional, certainly pastoral, rather than evangelical, chiliastic, or messianic. And we must remind ourselves of Dorothy Day's mystical side, her inclination to immerse herself in the mysteries of the Holy Spirit.

"Yes, we fail in love, we make our judgments and we fail to see that we are all brothers; we are all seeking love, seeking God, seeking the beatific vision." She is describing (in *Loaves and Fishes*) her experiences in jail, this time when she and others took their stand (in 1957) against "the yearly war game of taking shelter during the aid-raid drill." She was trying to tell the reader how she felt, locked up in Manhattan's Women's House of Detention. She was hoping to indicate why her pacifist principles moved her to do as she did and how she got along with her fellow demonstrators once behind bars. She was hoping to tell the reader about her lapses and faults, her episodes of pride and self-righteousness, her moodiness or abruptness. She was straining to indicate how fragile it all can be, the encounter of decently and honorably motivated Christian willfulness with man's psychological complexities and, never to be overlooked, society's capacity to make even the best-intentioned gestures seem vain, self-serving, barrenly theatrical. In despair, she had talked about herself with unusual candor and once again demonstrated the strongly emotional turn of her mind—even as that same mind struggled for scrupulously logical self-scrutiny, and even as she was ever willing to take up her own kind of arms, in carefully thought-out and carefully enacted ways, against a government that has stockpiled enough hydrogen bombs to kill everyone on this planet a dozen times over. (Do psychiatrists look into the minds of those who are proudly responsible for *that* kind of policy or act?)

The Catholic Worker movement became many things: an idea, a collection of people, a community, a growing tradition, a school, a scattering of places wherein good works are practiced, a set of aims and purposes, an instrument of God's will, an expression of His gracious presence within the context of history. Just as the movement is so various, its relationship to various segments of America's (and the world's) population, Catholic and non-Catholic, has fluctuated, often quite stormily. The paper's immediate success came as a surprise, but even more unexpected was the personal response that thousands of people made to the daily example offered by the movement, in the various hospitality houses. People were not only fed, clothed, but, not least, given psychological and spiritual counsel and support of the kind that social planners and the governments they influence often fail even to think about or consider important, let alone provide. Hundreds and hundreds of men and women volunteered their time, energy, resources, to help in that effort. Money poured in; the rich or merely comfortable were given a chance to unburden themselves, maybe even for a chance to feel closer to God than Mammon. The hurt, the lonely, the forsaken were given a home; the sick were attended—with all that such a phrase implies.

At this point, I have to indicate a little of what I have seen going on—what needs to be and is being done in a place like St. Joseph's House, on Manhattan's Lower East Side. For example, a woman comes in; she is very much to herself, looks about furtively; when someone approaches her (to say hello, to offer a cup of coffee) her body draws back, her face pales, her eyes are quickly lowered. In a moment she is sitting on a chair and looking beyond that room, into a distance no one else can fathom, at a landscape only she will ever see and experience. Suddenly, though, she is in pain. She cries out. She bends over and starts to scratch her leg, much of which is covered by a bandage. Now she is being approached again, and this time there is no withdrawal, no flight inward. Her leg moves an inch or two outward. It is not thrust forward, shown defiantly or petulantly. Not a word is spoken. A young woman bends over, looks at the bandages, indicates by the look that comes over her face that something is wrong, something needs to be done. The older woman gets up; for a second she hesitates, her face tightens; she looks down again—and in an astonishing reversal of mood begins to smile, says, "Good Lord, what a mess"; practically submits herself to the will of the younger woman, who encourages her to button up her coat because it is bitter cold outside. A minute or two later they are gone to Bellevue, where the badly infected lower leg, a "secondary symptom" of a chronic diabetic condition, is examined, cleansed, treated with antibiotics, and bandaged once again.

Back at St. Joseph's House the woman is left to her own resources, left to muse, mutter, listen to a radio near the chair she likes to use—all of which she very much wants and needs to do, so long as there are others nearby to nod, suggest with a glance that a cup of coffee is available. (She knows that coffee is always there, but needs the beckoning look from another person.) She can also find a certain pleasure in the annoyance some of the men visitors provide for her. A man comes by, for instance, and stares at her. She is brought back from her own staring—to look at him, look him up and down. No doubt she has some names for him, but she knows not to speak them. She reserves her curses for those no one in St. Joseph's House will ever see; maybe at times she simply has to shake her fist at fate, shout out briefly the sadness she feels, the loneliness she hasn't altogether accepted. Meanwhile, he is carrying on. Tall, burly, unshaven, he is dressed in unpressed pants that are too long and a shirt so wrinkled it no longer seems remarkable, simply a part of him, never to be lost. He has been protected from the winter by a sailor's navy-blue jacket, and now he begins to take it off, as if ready to stay for a while; then he thinks better of it, leaves it on, weaves his way across the room and stands there, moving to and fro yet not leaving his place, just wobbling while his feet decide where to go next. He looks at the coffee and the bowl filled with bread—light rye, dark rye, big pieces, small pieces. He seems both ready to lunge for it and a continent away.

A young man has been watching him since he entered, has filled a mug with coffee and moved the bread down the length of the long table so that it is near the mug. Now the men look at each other; the older man quickly looks away, toward the coffee, the younger man moves to a chair and pulls it out, a welcome. In a few seconds the coffee is being drunk; as for the bread, it seems to be too much for a stomach used to liquids. The man does, however, watch two other men as they not only take coffee but carefully cover their bread with margarine and eat it with obvious relish. Something in him stirs, a twinge of envy every child knows and not a few grownups: "I wish I had their appetite. Look at them, so hungry. I'm glad I'm not hungry." Soon, though, his "rivalry" no longer bothers him; he can rest easy, let his head drop, begin to feel sleep; he starts violently, becomes agitated, raises himself almost violently from the table, lurches toward the door; but he stops short of it, turns around, and gazes almost dreamily at several posters—which urge peace, cry for racial justice, proclaim one or another Gospel lesson. Everything seems to blur in his head, his eyes open and close, his brow wrinkles, he scratches his head, confused by the scene, by "them," by their generosity, by their ever so restrained movements toward him, their seeming acceptance of him, of anybody. And meanwhile there are those pictures and words on the wall, evidence, it would seem, of some larger design on the part of his hosts than he has any desire or capacity (then or maybe ever) to comprehend. He quickly makes the break, can be seen crossing the street as if he is having a fine time amusing himself on a country road with not a worry in the world.

The room at St. Joseph's House is almost always occupied by people, sometimes dozens and dozens of them, all every table can hold, and plenty standing. Morning coffee, then soup, then supper; day after day that rhythm works itself out. In the back, men and women labor; they have big pots and pans, food they have brought or been given, and most of all they have energy. Coffee is made and made; bread is all the time being sliced, served, moved here and there to suit a particular person who has managed to come in but seems able to do little else. Vegetables are cut, diced, thrown into soups. Peter Maurin was a French peasant; he knew what a thick soup can mean, can do. In the evening there are more formal meals—meat, spaghetti, whatever. Volunteers go about their work: young people, men, women, clergy, laity, students on leave from college and there for a few months, working people there for a day, a week, to be of help, to do what little a person can do. Through it all, people sit and talk, sit in stony silence, sit and gain strength or feel appeased or prepare for the outside or listen absorbed or casually watch.

Not everything goes smoothly. Efficiency is certainly not the point, and St. Joseph's House is not meant to be a sort of Salvation Army rescue operation. Rancor and hate and violence are not rare, and have to be subdued. A black man comes in, dazed, hungry; a white man, equally dazed and hungry, speaks his mind. Both are ready to fight. A woman comes in shouting, looking for someone, anyone to insult. A man pushes his way past the others in the line, demands coffee, denounces the people who give it to him, and unsatisfied with that demonstration, threatens the nearest person he can find his way to. An orator (no less than that) arrives, anxious to tell everyone at the house how foolish they are, the place is. Others, knowing they have been hoodwinked over and over again for as far back as memory lasts, become restless or all too still, indicating without speaking how little they can take for granted, how vulnerable to almost anyone's provocation they always feel.

Those more fortunate, those who come to give rather than receive, can also be touchy. Dorothy Day candidly referred to "our dissensions" in *The Long Loneliness*. She has not made too much of them, but neither has she shirked mentioning them; she has needed no training in psychology or psychiatry to appreciate how contagious bitterness and resentment can be and, just as important, how insidious and disarming pride can be. We have little trouble accounting for the condition of the "Bowery bums," the poor, the distraught; they have lost all pride, we feel sure, and throw themselves at almost anyone's feet, virtually sell their souls, convinced in any case that they have already lost them for good. For us who try to help, it is harder to look at our own situation. Even at our best we may get rather a lot of pleasure in going through the motions, fulfilling the responsibility allowed us—so as to feel good about our sacrifices, satisfied at the sight of our achievements. "Don't you feel great being Mr. Kind!" I once heard someone shout in St. Joseph's House. It was an unfair accusation—arbitrary, gratuitous, unkind. Still, one responds to it with more than rightful annoyance; there is a painful moment of recognition: yes, I am surely capable of being a smug, self-righteous Mr. Kind—indeed, every once in a while more that than anything else. "Nothing is ours. All we have to give is our time and patience, our love. How often we have failed in love, how often we have been brusque, cold, and indifferent." Needless to say, Dorothy Day has in mind not only the way the fortunate treat the damned (so to speak) but the way those who are taking part in a shared social, political, and religious struggle behave toward one another.

There are others, allies and those felt to be friends or, sometimes, half-friends. On Friday nights for a long time speakers have come to St. Joseph's House in New York. At the farm at Tivoli, up along the Hudson River, meetings, discussion groups, and conferences have been held over the years. Pride is not absent on those occasions either: the enemy seems big, strong, immovable; the hours are long; the results, even modest gains, not always forthcoming; suddenly the temptation is indulged and only later recognized for what it has been—an outburst, a lunge of sarcasm or, more deviously, a smirk of self-satisfaction, a scornful glance, legs crossed as a sign of unyielding self-assurance. Perhaps we know somewhere inside ourselves how limited every single one of us is, and of course that kind of awareness can become yet another excuse for inaction, self-flagellation, and, of all ironies, prideful introspection. Still, in this century Union Square and other places like it all over the world have been filled with men and women who have wanted to fight injustice passionately, even if in so doing they risk becoming murderously possessive of *their* approach, *their* mode of analysis and attack. I suspect that the deliberate modesty characterizing the political tactics of the Catholic Worker movement reflects not only the deep-seated pacifism of Dorothy Day and others who have been at her side, but their collective realization that no one, however devoutly Christian, can take for granted what might best be called generosity of spirit.

At one point in *Loaves and Fishes* Dorothy Day almost flaunts the self-pity she and others have had to learn to master: "The farm library is open to all our guests. Autographed copies of books by Maritain, Eric Gill, and Belloc disappear. A friend carved us some beautiful statues and crucifixes, and one night they were gone. Another friend gave us a tapestry, a copy of a famous painting. Someone looked upon it with desire, and it was gone, too. Living in common as we do, available to all, free to all, we expect these things to happen." To expect is not to lack disappointment when the apparently inevitable and unwelcome moment arrives—the thing is gone, and I am without a precious sight, an object I looked at with joy and was helped by to pray. "It takes some time to calm one's heart," she goes on, "which fills all too easily with irritation, resentment, and anger." What she falls back upon is "the quiet of the chapel, and looking around at the work done by those same men who caused the irritation."

I stress this darker side to the Catholic Worker movement not to distinguish it from other movements, but to indicate how great are the odds any such effort faces, however virtuous its purposes and its daily achievements. I once attended vespers at St. Joseph's House—held in the basement of the building on East First Street. They were a small and quiet group that evening, as they are most evenings, a few of the most faithful, most loyal. They read from the Bible and soon enough dispersed—there was more work to be done, food needing preparation, newspaper copy requiring attention, an accumulation of household chores to get out of the way. First I noticed how gentle and loving they were. Then I noticed how tired they seemed. Finally, as their voices rose to a phrase, fell back only to rise yet again and more insistently, I realized how embattled they felt; we could for all the world have been in a catacomb of Rome, and of course emperors and their cohorts are not the only enemies Christians have had.

"Saint Paul said that he did not judge himself, nor must we judge ourselves. We can turn to our Lord Jesus Christ, who has already repaired the greatest evil that ever happened or could ever happen." For many of her radical friends those words of Dorothy Day's, that response on her part to a universal psychological temptation, is hard, maybe impossible, to understand. A good number of her friends and sympathizers have failed to (have not wanted to) pay much attention to that strain in her temperament, that crucial aspect of the movement she helped found. Nevertheless, at a particular moment in history, *The Catholic Worker* struck a responsive chord in many thousands of Catholics; just as significant, it appealed to many others—Protestants and Jews, agnostics and atheists —who recognized the dangers a whole range of secular ideologies can present. What is more, when *The Catholic Worker* turned rather quickly (as was always intended, if things worked out) into a broad movement, even more non-Catholics found themselves attracted to it, especially in the face of what Stalin's regime became—a vicious police state, reactionary in the extreme. Nor did the pained neutrality assumed by *The Catholic Worker* toward both sides in the Spanish Civil War go unnoticed, by Catholics or non-Catholics. The former in large numbers were scandalized; the Republican government had repeatedly attacked the Spanish Church, taking away its privileges and, during the war, inflicting vengeance upon its members. As for liberal and radical non-Catholics, they could only note that *The Catholic Worker* was at least not rushing in a frenzy to uphold Franco—and it is hard today to convey how passionately the American Catholic Church mobilized itself on behalf of the rebel Franco and against the "red-atheists" of the Spanish government.

Even the unpopular and unrelenting pacifist stand that was taken by

Dorothy Day and her associates during the late 1930s and through the Second World War earned grudging respect from many proudly atheistic radicals, especially those of more anarchist persuasion. In earlier years they may have dismissed Peter Maurin and Dorothy Day as well-meaning reformers, severely limited by their strange and sentimental involvement with the Catholic Church —of all nonprogressive institutions. Yet here were these devout Catholics willing to take on the United States government. Here were Catholics who opposed the concentration camps for American citizens of Japanese descent, who would go to jail for opposing the cold war in the late 1940s and 1950s, even though it was a war directed at "atheistic communism." And, as the years mounted up and became decades, here was a radical movement that *lasted*. In the 1950s and 1960s Dorothy Day and her friends committed themselves as willingly and energetically to the civil-rights movement, to the cause of Cesar Chavez, to the peace movement (one more war to be protested!) as they had to the stunned, unemployed families of the 1930s. So it is at least understandable that this movement came to be admired by those who simply ignored or glossed over some of its tenets, prominent among them its core faith. Ironically, the thoughtful involvement of people like Jacques Maritain, Frank and Maisie Ward Sheed, Michael Harrington, Thomas Merton, the sincere interest of writers like W. H. Auden and Evelyn Waugh and Dwight MacDonald, may have had the same effect. In this country, prominence has a way of blotting out everything else; if the famous have found something valuable in a person, a place, an activity, that alone is believed to be sufficient cause for a kind of emulation that is as uncritical as it is momentary and faddish.

ITGOESWITHOUTSAYING that for Dorothy Day, for the men and women she has worked with most closely, year after year, there is nothing more important than the Church. As I now write, all her books are long out of print; but by the time this book appears *The Long Loneliness* will have come back to life (it should particularly interest many of today's women), and the same goes for *Loaves and Fishes*, which young activist students anywhere in the world can and will profit from reading. She herself has no wish to boast about her novel, *The Eleventh Virgin*, though it covers much the same ground that the early chapters of *The Long Loneliness* do, and might be of value to women of the 1970s who may have made "progress," in contrast to what went on fifty years ago, but who still have to fight for some of the values and dreams that legitimately obsess the characters in that book. What the novel lacks, naturally enough, is the explicit religious commitment that one finds in everything Dorothy Day wrote after her conversion, which followed the publication of the novel by four years. A book that she would *not* mind seeing reissued is, quite possibly, no more likely to attract many present-day publishers than the novel; it is called *Thérèse*, and it is a touching and devoted account of the other Saint Teresa's life—the Saint Thérèse known to millions as the Little Flower.

Many must wonder what Dorothy Day can possibly find so inspiring and important about that saint. She was no great reformer, no special champion of the poor, no burning prophet intent upon nothing less than the spiritual reawakening of the Church. She has had no following among intellectuals, within or without the Church. She was not herself one; she came up with no original ideas, wrote no books, devised no programs, founded no new orders. She died a young woman, a would-be nun, after having suffered a terrible illness, debilitating and unresponsive to medical treatment. She was racked with pain. She wasted away. She hemorrhaged badly. She begged God to take her, the sooner the better. If she did not lose faith outright, she was in despair, overwhelmed by the enormity of the suffering she had to bear. Toward the end, her death was expected almost hourly yet seemed to elude her and, as well, the saddened and no doubt frightened members of the austere order to which she aspired. After a while the scene began to have dramatic power, becoming an almost apocalyptic encounter between the devil (exacting the worst kind of suffering, so much that it amounted to torture, minute after minute, stretching over a seemingly limitless expanse of time), and the soul of a believing Christian resigned to suffer any fate, experience any hardship, if such be the will of God.

All of this Dorothy Day relates with obvious admiration. She has no interest in dressing up Thérèse, making her more acceptable to the upper middle-class liberals and radicals who have, in significant numbers, grown to respect the social and political activism of Dorothy Day. She has no inclination to explain Thérèse's behavior, analyze her personality, fit her response to her illness into some broader social or cultural context. Openly and unshamedly she marvels at the young woman's spirit, her toughness, her expanding vision of God's purposes, her acquiescence before Him, her Cross-like mixture of loneliness and confidence that soon enough even the most inexplicable and burdensome suffering will be redeemed. For Dorothy Day, Thérèse's life was meant to be yet another reminder of Christ's gift to us all: through Him, through His emergence from the dark, the rest of us are offered something unforgettable and permanent. If such is called the stuff of childish dreams, if sickly sentiment is felt to be overly evident, if this is claimed to be an aberrancy in her, a blind spot, a serious mistake will, I think, have been made. Much that makes up the essential nature and spirit of the Catholic Worker movement has to do *precisely* with the emphasis Dorothy Day has given to Thérèse, the Little Flower whom so many poor, illiterate, and impressionable (some, not necessarily non-Catholic people would say superstitious) men and women have held to be very dear and important.

Perhaps I can get at what Dorothy Day has signaled in *Thérèse* (and elsewhere, too) by referring, a little didactically, to her "relationship" to the Catholic Church. Many converts do not look upon the Church as an inheritance of sorts— to be lived with, called upon, attended as a matter of course. For them, as for Saint Paul, God has been surprisingly kind, and such good fortune must not be forgotten. As one reads Dorothy Day her gratitude does indeed come across;

she loves the Church passionately. Yet something else has to be mentioned, too. She has not merely chosen to be a communicant; the Church has suffused her life, possessed her, even as she no doubt at times feels quite naturally possessive about it. For her the Church lives as an institution and a faithful and sustaining companion, a teacher, a source of inspiration, a refuge, and, of course, as a tradition in constant jeopardy. She came to the Church not through Saint Thomas, but through Saint Augustine. Catholic novelists like Mauriac and Claudel have meant more to her than Catholic philosophers or theologians. She lived a tempestuous life before she became a Catholic, and has continued to do so afterward. At no point since she left home for the university has she ever looked upon herself as anything but one of the vast majority of people who are *not* influential, *not* rich, *not* high up in some cultural or intellectual scene. This is not to say that she has been without ambition. It is obvious that she has become a significant person in the history of this country—and one suspects that after her death her importance as a Catholic layman will increase, perhaps, in time, dramatically.

But whatever her mark upon the world, she has lived in a certain way, directed her concerns toward certain people, all the while insisting upon voluntary poverty for herself and paradoxically offering the poor all she can obtain from the well off. In *Thérèse*, the heart of those ideals, commitments, and involvements gets spelled out. In both her autobiographical books and in *House of Hospitality*, a concern for the poor comes across on every page, but in *Thérèse* a somewhat different line of thinking is to be found. The author seems less preoccupied with the hungry, the desperate, more interested in stressing that most of us, hungry not for bread but for faith, struggle to find self-respect and dignity in our own eyes—and before God. In the last chapter, she asks herself why she wrote this particular book. So much has been written about the Little Flower—articles, long essays, biographies, books for children, *Storm of Glory, Love Is My Vocation, Written in Heaven*; clearly, Thérèse was not lacking admirers. Why yet another book? She points out that writers like herself were not the ones who first responded to Thérèse: "It was the 'worker,' the common man, who first spread her fame by word of mouth. It was the masses who first proclaimed her a saint. It was 'the people'." Why? What in Thérèse's life appealed to the average Catholic believer?

> Perhaps because she was so much like the rest of us in her ordinariness. In her lifetime there are no miracles recounted, she was just good, good as the bread of their diet. Good as the pale cider which takes the place of the wine of the rest of France, since Normandy is an apple country. "Small beer," one might say. She compares to the great saints as cider compares with wine, others might complain. But it is the world itself which has canonized her, it is the common people who have taken her to their hearts. And now the theologians are writing endlessly to explain how big she was, and not little, how mature and strong she was, not childlike and dependent.

Ordinariness is the important quality for Dorothy Day. *The Catholic Worker* was meant to address plain, ordinary working-men and -women who are Catholic or who respond to Christ's teachings. She never wanted to lose contact with these people; never wanted to lead them, either, or tell them they were being tricked, duped, fooled—and so, by implication, tell them they were dumb and gullible; never wanted to look upon herself as knowing, as "mature" and "responsible," an example to the benighted, illusion-saddled "masses" who needed to be uplifted by their betters. It is no accident that she follows her most pointed description of Thérèse and those who have venerated her with a somewhat ironic, if not mocking or sarcastic, comment about the effort of theologians to build the Little Flower up, make her a clever and thoughtful person, worthy of the Church's decision to decree her a saint. Radical as Dorothy Day has been, she has never wanted to sever her connections with those who don't think, let alone act or, more broadly, live as she does, but who submit to life's everyday demands (all too desperately, she would surely acknowledge, if pressed on the matter).

Once I spent the better part of a morning and an afternoon talking with her, and throughout her conversation she would not stop mentioning her concern for factory workers, machinists, construction workers, clerks—the people called "blue-collar workers" or "white-collar workers" by those who are neither. She talked about them without condescension, without rancor, without disappointment. At no time were they the noble proletarians some of her friends of the early 1920s had held them up to be, and they were not now the narrow, mean-spirited people, the collective menace which some who share her political passions insist on calling them. When the subject came up for about the tenth time, she turned in her chair and suddenly her rather dark room lit up with her impatience, her annoyance—if not outright anger: "I have never expected, I have never wanted everyone to become part of the Catholic Worker family. We are small, necessarily so. This is not for everyone—this life, this way of doing things. It would be awful if we started looking down on people who are different, who are called upon to live lives so different from ours. I've never wanted to lecture to people; I've hoped to act in such a way that I will be reaching out to many others who will never be part of the Catholic Worker movement." A little later on, as if to emphasize that point, she told me how much time she has spent looking at, hearing, trying to understand and feel close to working-men and -women: "I used to sit in Grand Central Station and watch people by the hour, until often a policeman would come and ask me just what I was doing there! I love riding the bus; I can listen to people talking, learn what they are thinking and hoping to do. One can get isolated from such people when one is in a 'movement.' We started *The Catholic Worker* in order to address millions of fellow Catholics, many of whom had the same ideas we did, but no one saying them out loud. I have never wanted to be far away from the ordinary working people I sit beside in church."

She has succeeded in that regard. She has repeatedly made it plain that in the Church she found a kind of transforming and sustaining love which perhaps defies the wordy comprehension of the intellectuals she has both felt drawn to and anxious to part company with. She has not, however, written or talked much about another aspect of her relationship to Rome—which concerns the *discipline* of the Church. At first glance the Catholic Worker movement does not seem especially disciplined; many of its members are virtually anarchist, many at the least have fought against the various routines and schedules, life-consuming as they are, that advanced capitalist societies impose upon their members. The hospitality houses may strike a visitor as casually run, if not chaotic: people come and go, vague as to what they want or need—and are not pressed hard by those in attendance. Yet the men and women who work in those houses are very much in attendance; all the time they attend to hunger and pain, disorder and sorrow. To do so, to look after so many of the homeless, bereft, exceptionally needy, to feed them, to fit them with clothes, to arrange for their medical care and to pray for them, to act on their behalf in various kinds of demonstrations, to write about their fate, to bring the importance of their suffering lives to the attention of the many thousands who for some forty years have read *The Catholic Worker*—all of that requires restraint, tact, an organizer's ability to be ready and waiting at just the right moment.

Day in, day out, the food is there, always on time; and those who wait in line for clothes are not disappointed, or asked to disperse and come back *maybe* tomorrow, or *sometime* next week. Schedules are followed, troubled and often enough vague or elusive people are kept after—their medicine has to be taken, their bandages changed, even though they have managed all too long to take advantage of the world's indifference, not to mention their own, directed against themselves. Dorothy Day and her co-workers are antidotes to that indifference; if anything they have tried to be relentlessly, tenaciously *there*, prepared for any eventuality known to a certain kind of modern man or woman. They are prepared to wait, in many instances until they themselves are helpless and ready to die, with little expectation that their labors as Catholic laymen will produce dramatic or even remotely measurable results—in their lives or in the lives they seek to meet and help repair. And they are prepared psychologically to be both practical and devoutly religious, preoccupied with the things of this world but unable to forget the promise of a "life everlasting." All of this requires balance and discipline: an allegiance to a coherent, summoning point of view that satisfies the mind and heart, and engages successfully with the will, exacting the day-to-day labor that converts ideas (or, more grandly, ideologies) into ongoing social and political effort.

The Catholic Worker movement, as its name declares, is a movement aimed at workers, a movement that hopes to speak for them *as workers*. It is not primarily concerned with Catholic family life, or Catholic culture, or Catholic theology, or Catholic education—though all of those issues cannot be ignored. The emphasis is on man or woman the doer, the producer, the person intent on making his or her way, the individual who has tried to find a place in the world's scheme of things. The emphasis is on the large part of our lives that, for most of us in the West, starts after breakfast and ends in the late afternoon before suppertime. We are asked to consider what kind of working life we have today and what kind we might have if the world were more decent, just, and, not least, Christian in actuality. We are asked to consider how vulnerable the average workingman is, at the mercy not only of factory owners and managers, but of the values and ideals a nation insists upon. What Simone Weil saw as killing French factory workers and threatening its peasants, Dorothy Day and Peter Maurin founded a political and social movement to fight against: a world in which man has become the digit, the bribed Rotarian or Optimist, the applauded Stakhanovite.

The "message" of that movement (if such it has to be called) has remained remarkably alive and in tune with the worries and aspirations of several, very different generations of Americans. In the 1930s Dorothy Day and Peter Maurin spoke on behalf of the millions without work and food. They stressed the horror of conditions, the gross injustice such a state of affairs amounted to, but at the same time they took pains to remind their readers that theirs was a vision far different from some political pragmatist's or economic reformer's—and the 1930s spawned many of each. Theirs was a vision tied to the Church, and tied, vaguely yet specifically, to an amalgam of convictions and passions that Dorothy Day has characteristically never seen fit to formulate with any great precision or insistence, perhaps because a mystical element intervenes (as is the case with some of her heroes, like Dostoevski and Tolstoi) which is not entirely a reflection of religious sensibility. Still, repeated statements after a while reveal preoccupations, and with some hesitancy I want to indicate what I believe distinguishes the Catholic Worker movement from other social-reformist groups, even those tied to the Catholic Church. For one thing, as I have already mentioned, there is the unfailing concern for ordinary working-men and -women, matched by an equally emphatic involvement in the life they live. Non-elitist, I suppose one could say. No elaborate proposals are handed down from on high to be "implemented" by other people.

In other words, we are not dealing with a movement of intellectuals or upper-middle-class professional people who are disenchanted with capitalist America and desire changes for themselves, and by the same token, for others. Obviously, intellectuals started the movement and have been attracted to it all along. Obviously, some very well-to-do people have been moved to support it and in doing so have found a whole new way of thinking about the world. Yet, if the Catholic Worker movement has come to anything, it has been by virtue of its steadfast refusal to allow a certain *essence* to be separated from the demands that *existence* puts on social philosophies as much as individual personalities. One has in mind not only old-fashioned aphorisms like "practice what you preach," but even more broadly, the faith Dorothy Day places in the slow, unostentatious drift of life. She accords great importance to *becoming*. We not only *are,* we not only stand for this or that and live in such-and-such a way, but have within us a whole range of possibilities or potentialities, often unacknowledged, even unknown. Given a chance for expression, they might emerge and make us different, a little bit so, or altogether so, in which case Saint Paul's description of "new men" might be considered applicable. Unquestionably, those in the Catholic Worker movement make up a religious community, but they also are a band of *workers*. They have chosen to seek after their ideals in a manner that makes the search a living experiment. Since they worship God, they can never take for granted their condition as "new men"—hence the tentativeness and uncertainty, the tendency to modesty and humility in people who nonetheless know what they believe and what they want to do.

Life-style is the issue, to draw upon the modern expression. When Peter Maurin and Dorothy Day rather quickly decided that the paper they founded and edited was a mere beginning, a prelude to the further development of hospitality houses and farms, they in effect turned their back on many of the Union Square people they knew so well. They wanted to live with those they hoped to help, eat and sleep alongside those they wanted to stimulate with editorials or "easy essays" or remarks written while "on pilgrimage." And since they were to be involved with the poorest of the poor, the least educated, and maybe the most hurt psychologically in our society, they must have known that such a commitment was a lasting one. Not for them a protest here, a statement of outrage there. Not for them a carefully planned meeting, or a summer's political activity, followed by a resumption of "things as they are." Not even for them the more sustained commitments made by other activists: years and years of petitions signed, essays written, assertions made and refined and clarified and argued over and defended, often at great personal cost. Dorothy Day did not help to establish St. Joseph's House of Hospitality because she felt some of her old Socialist and Communist friends were failing to put their lives on the line, or were coming forth with nothing more than fancy talk. She knew that they were principled and self-sacrificing, and she never was tempted to repudiate them as friends, attack them, or suggest that her various decisions ought at some moment become theirs. She and others simply found that for themselves writing and political action were but a part of a larger kind of life, and they went about their business—locating places to live, learning what kind of food was best to serve others and eat themselves, finding out how people who have gone to college and who read books and write articles can *live together*, in all the senses of the expression, how they can get on, feel one another's affection and support, do so despite the inevitable moments of disenchantment, envy, jealousy, resentment.

To understand the movement one must look into how these many people have lived together, under what conditions and for what purposes. "Voluntary poverty": often Dorothy Day uses those words. In her youth she fought poverty, but in the last four decades of her life she took it on and found it a blessing. At this point the reformist spirit of the movement—the alliance with workers as they struggled to unionize, the loyalty to men like Martin Luther King, and Cesar Chavez and the causes they have represented—confronts other values constantly emphasized in *The Catholic Worker:* a pastoral inclination; a distrust of urban-industrial and commercial life as it exists in both capitalist or state socialist nations; a long-standing interest in the quality of the environment, ranging from the air we breathe, the water we drink, the land we live on and grow food on, to details like how a newspaper gets illustrated, how a house of hospitality is set up, how furniture is used, food prepared, religious rituals practiced.

Contemporary words, with all that they imply, warrant mention—ecology, communes, consumerism. It is possible to go through old issues of *The Catholic Worker,* and through Dorothy Day's books as well, and emerge with the impression that a group of naturalists have somehow stumbled into twentieth-century politics while never really forsaking their first love, the unspoiled land—which ought to be shared and indeed loved, perhaps second only to God Himself. The smallest animal, the least bush or flower, a stretch of the shore, the rise of a hill, a section of a forest, none is ignored by her and her co-authors, even as the reader is urged to think of the world-shaking struggles that catch up various classes and nations. Nor are the clear and powerful woodcuts that grace *The Catholic*

Worker a fortuitous but ideologically insignificant accident. From Saint Francis of Assisi to Eric Gill, certain Catholics have found evidence of God in nature and, by the same token, have felt a responsibility to enhance the world's beauty—positively, through various acts of creation, and indirectly, by insisting upon certain moral and aesthetic standards. In that spirit one shuns waste, extravagance, gaudy and ornate excesses. In that spirit one is not ascetic or puritanical—austere, maybe, but not austere for the sake of austerity but rather out of loving respect for what God has created. Now presumably He has to watch His world desecrated: by smog, spillage, billboards; by brazenly colonialist industrial parks and sprawling settlements, put down anywhere and everywhere, the devil with the cost to the countryside; and, too, by slick and glossy publications, produced at God knows what cost and for God knows what purpose. (One must invoke both the devil and God because in the Catholic Worker movement the issue really does come down to that.)

By the same token, the relationship of the hospitality houses to the streets they front is remarkable; new buildings have not been erected, no matter how much money is contributed to the movement, nor are hours announced in which one "service" is done, followed later on by the next. Students of "organizational behavior" would doubtless note a certain "fluidity" between the outside and the inside. Where does St. Joseph's House begin or end? At which side of a door that is always open? At the edge of the small rear garden? People come and go, day and night. People have to stay, be bedded, even if there is not enough space. People have to get out of the city, need to be at the farm at Tivoli for a while. No "staff discussions" are held to make "decisions." No "hierarchical structure" is, step by step, "consulted." Time and space are "fluid"; people with their moments of need, of pain, of indecision, of happiness, and of devotion, meet and come to some terms with each other and move on. It is a kinetic, emotional, often unpredictable atmosphere. A newspaper is written and edited, then addressed and mailed. A soup kitchen is maintained. A psychiatrist, if he feels under the compunction to do so, might say that it is a "half-way house," in which people who can barely manage outside of mental hospitals are given "support." One day Mass is held; the next day a lecture is given. I guess it even could be argued, quite convincingly, that "multiphased training programs" are constantly being offered. College students come to offer their energy and idealism and to learn about things their textbooks have ignored. Priests or nuns come to look or work. Foreign observers drop by. As Dorothy Day has remarked many times (and she is always puzzled by the fact), one can never really predict who is going to be there and be as quickly gone, and who is going to stay a lifetime—appropriately enough, since she herself never expected, back in 1933, to establish a movement that cut across the activities which words like social welfare, religion, medicine, psychiatry, education, journalism, political action are intended to suggest.

The constant and inevitable tension within the Church between its prophetic and pastoral roles most certainly is to be found in this lay group. On one hand, Dorothy Day, Peter Maurin, Ammon Hennacy, and others have written at considerable length (in *The Catholic Worker* and elsewhere) about what is wrong with our society and what needs to be done if we are to live in a kinder, more decent, and more compassionate country; on the other hand, day after day those who live and work in hospitality houses all over the country tend to the immediate needs which countless men and women bring in some hope of fulfillment. Christ the prophet denounced the rich, the powerful, the corrupt, the cold of heart and legalistic of mind; Christ the healer cared for those who required and wanted bread, a physician's hand, the sanction of one who was not interested in judging, but rather touching, affirming, redeeming. Christ the teacher gave us the beatitudes. Christ the worker walked and walked, responding always and in the most daring and unconventional manner to people whom educated and influential figures chose to ignore or regard with contempt. Only the most categorical theologian would want to subsume one of those two directions of concern and action under the other, and only a similar kind of observer would want to emphasize the political and social activism of the Catholic Worker family at the expense of its stubbornly attentive regard for the individuals who have urgent reasons to come knocking, looking, asking.

I SAID IN THE INTRODUCTION to this book that I could only offer my own particular response to the Catholic Worker movement. I have tried to refrain from discussing my personal experiences with the movement—there being quite enough to record of other people's words and deeds. But as I near the end of this essay, I want to acknowledge some of those moments. The earliest go back to my childhood, times when as a young boy I sat near a Philco radio and listened with my mother and father to Father Charles Coughlin, and heard them comment with sorrow on the frustrated, reactionary character of his Catholic populism. "The Church deserves better, we all deserve better," my father would say, and yet he would not stop listening—because, as he told me recently, when I asked why: "The man, in his own wrong-headed way, was pointing out the Church's social gospel at a time when that gospel was badly needed, and so much of the Church was silent." Still, the 1930s also gave us Dorothy Day and Peter Maurin, and I heard of them as a boy, was told that they were trying to follow the teachings of Christ, pay allegiance to Him not with words but deeds. "Our Protestant and Catholic churches bury Christ rather than serve Him." I heard that often enough from my parents; one of the few qualifying phrases would be "—except for *The Catholic Worker*, its kind of people," and I would quickly be told that they were in a manner of speaking outside the Church, "only members, not policy makers."

There is no doubt about that; Dorothy Day has not sat in any chancery offices deciding what shall or shall not be said in the name of Christ's Holy Roman Catholic Church. And she has not, as some secular, radical activists may have wished, taken to protesting the Church's position on various issues. A vigorous critic of corporate, bureaucratic capitalism (private or state, it makes little difference), she has submitted willingly to Cardinals as her spiritual leaders, even if she has disagreed with what they say about a particular war, or indeed a whole range of social issues. It is uncanny how loyal she can be to an institution whose authorities must at times have deeply offended her. Some would say her position is untenable, but she is a religious woman, and the Catholic Worker movement aims to fight for possession of the Christian Church, even as Saint Paul did. Like Bernanos and Mauriac, she knows how often the Church betrays Christ, becomes His greatest (most disedifying, most scandalous) burden. Nevertheless, one prays, remains faithful—and again, fights. I have heard a good deal about that paradox over the years, and enough of what I heard was illustrated with mention of the Catholic Worker movement to make me seek out first Dorothy Day's writings, then a hospitality house in Boston, and eventually St. Joseph's House in New York, where she lives and works.

Most significant of all for me has been a continuing friendship with a few members of the movement whom I met in the early 1960s, when they were involved in the civil-rights struggle in the South, as was I. During the most uncertain and uneasy and dangerous moments of that struggle in 1963, 1964, and 1965—the Mississippi Summer Project, the various marches led by Dr. King—it was enormously helpful to know and spend time with the young people who had worked at St. Joseph's House and felt themselves to be part of the Catholic Worker tradition. Here is one of them, then twenty-three years old and living near Greenwood, in Mississippi's Delta; I believe she will tell the reader a number of things about herself and the Catholic Worker movement:

"I'm not even Catholic, but I'm a Catholic Worker. It was my uncle who told me about *The Catholic Worker*. He reads it. He'd give it to us to read. His wife is a Catholic. She's a wonderful woman, my aunt is. She was a suffragette, like Dorothy Day; she went to jail fighting for the vote. . . . When I went East from Minnesota on a trip, they told me to go visit Thirty-six East First Street. I said why, because I only wanted to see my friends. It was a couple of years later that I decided to do it, and since then I've never been the same. It may sound arrogant to you, but I truly wish there was more of the spirit of the Catholic Worker movement in *this* movement. I'm not trying to set up Dorothy Day as a saint (she is, but not in the way a lot of people say she is) and I'm not trying to say there hasn't been a lot of trouble and friction and fighting in every hospitality house. People read something Dorothy Day writes, and if they're interested they might come by and visit St. Joseph's House, and see the 'Bowery bums' being fed, and then they say: 'It's wonderful, she's wonderful, it's the nicest place, with all those kind Christian people being so good, so extra-special good, to the poor.' They'd like to cover us with sugar coating and make us a big, harmless cake, sitting there for the poor to come and eat.

"Meanwhile there's Dorothy and a lot of others, and let me tell you, they are tough and shrewd and they've been around and they are fighters, not just sweet people who pray for the poor and go a step further by offering them coffee and soup. I never knew how much I learned from the Catholic Worker people until I came down here. . . .

"I guess things have worked out well for me here because I was brought up in the Mid-West and given *The Catholic Worker* to read; I guess it's because I'm not from an upper-middle-class, agnostic, intellectual background and going to an Ivy League school. I shouldn't talk like that; I'm the snob now! But I'll have to admit, I'm tired of people coming down here (orthodox atheists, they are!) and looking at these people as if they're nothing, absolutely nothing—as if they haven't built up for themselves values and ideals, even if they don't read *Deep South,* and all the textbooks, but just figure out everyday how to live with 'the man,' how to take care of each other, and how to look up to God and pray to Him and not be looking at themselves all the time instead.

"I've talked about some of these things; I'd better say *argued.* They tell me I'm sentimental, and I'm 'going Southern agrarian,' and I'm mystical, and I'm 'romanticizing' the poor. Dorothy would smile; if she were here she'd smile. She's known these people—their fathers and mothers—all her life; she'll say she was one of them long ago, a liberal or radical intellectual. But she couldn't have been, not really. Anyway, if she was here she'd smile and listen and say very little. She'd just go about doing the work—and not be too surprised, I believe, at what she saw. She'd love the people and the land and the way they pitch in and help each other. She'd love their faith, their plain old good manners with each other. They're country people, that's what they are, black and white; they know a lot of what Peter Maurin and Dorothy Day believe in, because they're attached to the land, and they love to do things for themselves, and they have their own idea of how to keep a cabin, shaky as it is, poor as they are, looking nice, 'pleasing to the eye,' they say: 'we want to keep things pleasing to the eye, even if we don't have much to be pleased with around here, what with the white man and his strutting around.'

"I could take *The Catholic Worker*, issue after issue, and show you how the things that we were preoccupied with in St. Joseph's House are the things the people here in the Delta are preoccupied with. They leave to go to the cities because they're desperate, but they know better. They don't want to end up torn from each other, wandering in those mazes of Harlem or Chicago's South Side. They'd like to see each man able to make a living, have his farm. They'd like to keep praying, keep up all those involvements with dozens of kinfolk, neighbors, and friends—it's a community they have, geographical and blood-wise and religious and economic. They're always rescuing each other, giving each other lifts—not in cars, because they mostly don't have them, but with food or a 'message,' they'll call it, which means a prayer, a reminder that all is not that bad, because 'the Lord provides'; and they don't *believe* that, they *experience* it as a living kind of truth. . . .

"The people here are struggling for more than the vote; their rescuers, *us*, want them to 'enter the political process.' But they have a vision of life, a philosophy they've built up through the years of suffering—and watching, and keeping on their toes, and keeping their eyes and ears open, and lifting their heads up to the sky in prayer. Sure, they want to be rescued, though not just so they can go to that courthouse and check a ballot. . . . Dorothy and the Negro people here have another kind of life to think about; Jesus Christ gave His life so that their lives, our lives, could be redeemed, and she's trying to live up to that sacrifice, prove herself worthy of it, and so are the people here. That's what I mean; that's why I say I was prepared for coming down here. That's why I'm at home here."

One need not uphold every word of this, or for that matter, every word of Dorothy Day's, to appreciate the special perspective they both offer. It is unlikely that the Catholic Worker movement—its newspaper, its intricate and binding web of people and places and activities, the strange mixture of a religious and social and cultural and political-activist tradition it has become—will change American society in any deep-seated or "structured" way. Moreover, those who belong to the movement tend not to be oracular, argumentative, or ideological— maybe because they really do believe God has already shown Himself (and His design) to us, maybe because they are not the socially prominent, the highly educated, the most ambitious and accredited members of our society, or maybe out of God's grace. All that can be said is that for forty years thousands of people have in numerous and different ways felt themselves to be part of a family of sorts: have given to one another, received from one another, learned from one another, and, especially, worked and prayed for one another.

There came a time in Mississippi when many of the agnostic and well-educated youths who contributed to the civil-rights movement began to see what this young "Catholic worker" was about, what possessed her, so to speak. The black people of Mississippi taught those well-to-do Yankee students much of what she had learned in Manhattan and at the Catholic Worker farm at Tivoli. The students were not "converted"; the Catholic Worker movement is not interested in proselytizing, and as for the South's black sharecroppers, they are supposed to need saving themselves. No, it simply happened that these students lived long enough and in such a way that a blessed moment came when they felt able to turn on themselves, look at their own assumptions and preconceptions, find for themselves a wider notion of what it is to be a human being on this earth.

Some of us spend a lifetime avoiding that kind of confrontation with ourselves. We regard critically just about everyone we meet, certainly if they threaten us with a different view of man's obligations and responsibilities; and all the while we don't think, don't want to ask ourselves what finally we believe. The poor and oppressed blacks of rural Mississippi showed their Northern friends that they had within themselves a continuing, at times a grim and feverish, faith—not as blacks or Southerners or Americans, but as children of God. Their Northern friends were not by and large about to join up, but they were ready to feel less cynical, maybe a touch envious—and since it seemed strange and even bizarre to envy sharecroppers and tenant farmers, a young member of the Catholic Worker family became the object of curiosity and, slowly, respect. "She knows them and they know her; they understand each other," I heard. Surprise eventually yielded to comprehension—I suppose the young activists came to comprehend a little of what Dorothy Day's "on pilgrimage" is about, because in their own way they, too, had become pilgrims that summer.

Since I was myself one of them, I have found it hard to shake off what it meant to read *The Long Loneliness* in places like Humphrey or Leflore counties, Mississippi. I carried the book with me to McComb, where a number of us very nearly met up with the end of our particular time in Mississippi—and elsewhere. And a little while later I found myself in a correspondence with Dorothy Day, which in turn prompted this book.

Often I have tried to summarize for myself what it is she and Peter Maurin together initiated, nourished, and gave to so completely. I have also wondered what the Catholic Worker movement has become, or perhaps I should say *is becoming*. Since 1933, good works have been done, wrongs been condemned, social and political justice urged, faith in God maintained and given the flesh of daily affirmation—deeds done in its name. Presidents, prime ministers, kings, and dictators have paid no attention. A New Jerusalem has not appeared. Millions of children continue to crave food, continue to sit fearfully expecting death —their bellies bloated, their eyes dazed, and, no doubt like the philosophers that every century provides, their minds haunted by eternal what's and why's and when's: what does all this mean, and why do such things happen, and when will men and women begin treating other men and women decently and kindly? Wars have been followed by more wars. Bombs have gotten bigger, more deadly, and those who order them used come up with the same, slippery, crafty words to justify their actions—rhetorical, simple-minded abstractions, ingratiating self-justifications, grandiose efforts to call upon history if not God Himself in the name of murder. Mediocre men, or brazenly egotistical men, ingenious men given to lies and conspiracies, dominate not a few of the world's nations. Somewhere, Isaiah must still be crying. Every day Christ is crucified—by those who dare to call upon Him as they sign proclamations, pull levers, go before their countrymen plaintively or with swagger to demand compliance while war goes on, and indifferent policies are pursued.

In the face of this history, one is hard put to rejoice in the achievements of Dorothy Day and her co-workers in the Catholic Worker movement. All they ever wanted to do was declare, affirm, signify, and act upon their individual and collective faith—at once a faith in the God of the prophets and the God of the apostles. They themselves have become prophets of sorts, and also apostles of that Nazarene who was drawn to the outcast and lowly of a great empire. A spectacle to the world of the first century, Paul and his brother Christians became; a spectacle to our world Dorothy Day and her brothers and sisters in the Catholic Worker movement have become. Without shame they have displayed courage, determination, love of Christ and His people—all of them, all of us. Without fear they have gone forth and met their neighbors more than half way, the despised and scorned and injured. Some spectacles can be gaudy extravaganzas, showy scenes. In that sense of the word, the spectacle of the world's condition, a continuing, scandalous betrayal of life, flagrantly dressed up in pieties and called "progress" or "civilization"—has yet again been shown for what it is by a small band of believing Christians. One can only be thankful—and feel obliged to commit that gratitude to a kind of work that is worthy of what the Catholic Worker movement has done and continues to do.

DATE